Dear Reader,

Welcome to the Pioneer Edition in the series of *Great Lakes Romances®* historical fiction full of love and adventure set in bygone days on North America's vast inland waters.

Like the other books in this series, *Elizabeth of Saginaw Bay* relays the excitement and thrills of a tale skillfully told, but contains no explicit sex, offensive language, or gratuitous violence.

We invite you to tell us what you would like most to read about in *Great Lakes Romances®*. For your convenience, we have included a survey form at the back of the book. Please fill it out and send it to us.

At the back, you will also find descriptions of other romances in this series, and a biography in the *Bigwater Classics*tm series, stories that will sweep you away to an era of gentility and enchantment, and places of unparalleled beauty and wonder!

Thank you for being a part of *Great Lakes Romances®!*

Sincerely,
The Publishers

P.S. Author Donna Winters loves to hear from her readers. You can write her at P.O. Box 177, Caledonia, MI 49316.

Elizabeth of **Saginaw Bay**

Donna Winters

Great Lakes Romances®

Bigwater Publishing
Caledonia, Michigan

First Published 1986: Zondervan Publishing House, Grand Rapids, Michigan
Newly edited and reprinted by Bigwater Publishing

Great Lakes Romances is a registered trademark of Bigwater Publishing,
P.O. Box 177, Caledonia, Michigan 49316.

Library of Congress Catalog Card Number: 94-78723
ISBN 0-923048-83-9 (Previously ISBN 0-310-47272-5)

This novel is a work of fiction. Names, characters, places, and incidents are either the product of the author's imagination or, if real, are used fictitiously.

Edited by Pamela Quint Chambers
Cover art by Patrick Kelley

Printed in the United States of America

95 96 97 98 99 00 01 /   / 10 9 8 7 6 5 4 3 2 1

To my mother
Frances Elizabeth Patte Rogers

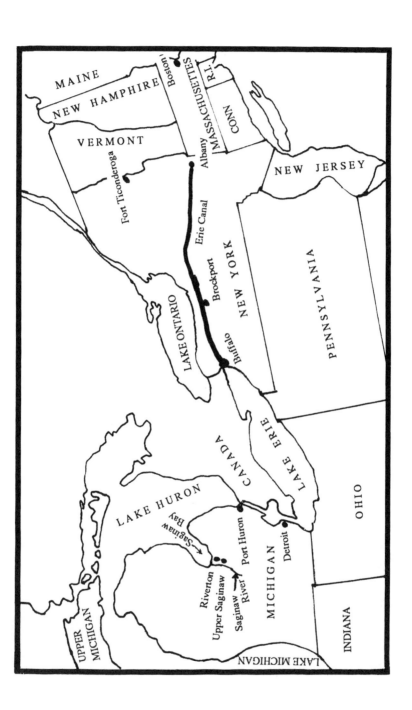

CHAPTER

1

Saginaw Valley, Michigan
July 1, 1837

Shock set in as twenty-year-old Elizabeth Morgan gripped the scarred rail of the *Governor Marcy* and searched the untamed eastern bank of the Saginaw River for the town she was now to call home. Where were the streets, the clapboard houses, the picket fences?

A small dock gave evidence of civilization. Above it, shin tangle, wild roses, and morning glories—closed tight in the waning of the hot afternoon—spread a rude carpet up either side of a split rail stairs. At the top of a three-foot slope, a needle-strewn path entered a daunting pine and hardwood forest. There, amongst towering trees, Elizabeth could barely make out a primitive settlement of squat log cabins, and the shadowy figure of a man standing at the head of a trail.

Could this possibly be Riverton, the village in which

Elizabeth and her new husband, Jacob, had invested nearly all of the wedding gift his father had bestowed on them? She drew a sharp breath. The essence of pine tempered the stench of the steamer's green wood smoke, but couldn't quell her panic, nor sweeten the taste of anxiety on her tongue. As Captain Winthrop gave a final blast of the steam whistle and shouted commands to make fast, she looked frantically for her husband.

The six-foot-tall, thirty-year-old, third-generation banker was at the bow, white shirt sleeves rolled up as he helped a crusty crewman secure the vessel to the pier. Elizabeth made haste for the front of the steamer, but before she reached Jacob, he leaped over the gunwale.

Jacob raced up the riverbank steps two at a time, almost certain the hefty figure at the top would be his father's brother. His suspicion proved true when his uncle emerged in full sunlight waving his broad-brimmed hat furiously.

"Nephew! Welcome!"

"Uncle Will! Good to see you again!" As Jacob embraced his uncle, he suppressed his own anxiety—and a multitude of questions—about the idyllic town which had been described in correspondence. But Jacob would take up the matter later. Right now, his purpose would be better served by allowing time to reunite himself with the relative he hadn't seen in two years—his only acquaintance within five hundred miles.

Elizabeth watched as Jacob hugged Uncle Will, and wondered how her husband could put his arms about the scoundrel who had convinced him that the best investment on earth was the thriving town that in reality did not exist. They were talking animatedly as they made their way to the dock, and she hoped Jacob was petitioning for a return of his investment.

Her thoughts were disrupted by a scuffling on the deck, and she saw that the crewman was heading for the gangway, her curve-topped trunk balanced on his broad shoulders.

"Stop! Bring that back!" she cried, hurrying to catch up with him. "Return that trunk to my cabin. I'm not getting off here."

"But this here's your stop, ma'am. Riverton," insisted the fellow, tapping a grimy knuckle against the bold letters Jacob had painted on the side of the trunk.

Before she could argue further, he trudged down the gangway and deposited her trunk on the dock—at the feet of Jacob and his uncle.

Jacob gazed up at her, beckoning with his wide, captivating smile and a wave of his arm. "Elizabeth, come down here. I want to introduce you to someone."

Wondering how he could accept the situation with such equanimity, she gripped the rail with both hands, leaned forth, and stated firmly, "I'm not getting off this boat, Jacob."

His smile faltered as he tossed his head, shaking the sun-gold hair from his heavenly blue eyes, and started up the gangway. Wrapping his large, strong hands about her tiny wrists, he leaned down and spoke softly in her ear. "Elizabeth, my darling, you know I'd never leave you on this boat, don't you?"

"But Jacob—"

He cut short her protestation. "Don't fret, my precious." Blowing a kiss into her ear, he whispered, "I love you madly. I'm only asking you to do what's best. Now trust me and come meet Uncle Will."

Jacob's seductive goading, coupled with the enticing summer-fresh scent of him, weakened her resolve. Miffed by the ease with which she allowed him to lead her ashore, she refused to smile at the bearded man whose hazel eyes glimmered with a hint of mischief.

Will reached out, enfolding her hands in his huge, rough ones. "Elizabeth, welcome to the thriving community of Riverton! It's plain to me that the finest town in the Midwest has just been graced—"

"The finest town in the Midwest?" she challenged, jerking her hands free, then waving off a swarm of pesky mosquitoes.

Despite her sharp remark, his wide smile never faded, hinting at the source of her own husband's affable nature. "Like I was saying, the finest town in the Midwest has just been graced by the arrival of the most splendid-looking lady in all of York State!" He kissed her cheek before she could dodge the affection. "Now come with me. There are folks I want you to meet, and places you'll want to see." He headed up the steps.

Elizabeth spoke quietly to Jacob. "I've already seen all I want to." She started to turn toward the boat, but he prevented her, wrapping his arm about her waist.

"Be patient, my darling, and come along with me for now." Giving her a reassuring squeeze, he offered no choice but to go with him up the stairs.

Several adults and a passel of children had gathered atop the riverbank, and Uncle Will made introductions. "These here are the Farrells, the Sayers, the Langtons, and the Reverend and Mrs. Clarke." To those gathered, he said, "I'd like you all to make my nephew and his new bride feel welcome—Mr. and Mrs. Jacob Morgan, all the way from

Brockport, New York."

Elizabeth paid little attention to the names, certain she wouldn't be in Riverton long enough to bother getting to know all the men, women, and children Uncle Will had introduced so quickly. But the names of two women stuck in her mind as each of them shook her hand.

One was Mrs. Langton, whose thin, deeply lined face spoke of hardships and troubles. Her scrutinizing gaze put Elizabeth on edge, as did her bony handshake.

By contrast, Mrs. Clarke's genial, round face held a peace and serenity that seemed somehow familiar. When her plump hands enfolded Elizabeth's, she felt not only welcome, but as if the older woman was already a friend.

"Do come to my cabin for tea once you've settled in," said Mrs. Clarke. "You'll know our place by the wooden cross on the door."

"You're so kind," Elizabeth replied, about to explain she'd be gone on the morrow. But Jacob's uncle took her by the hand and led her away.

"I'm sure you're anxious to get to your honeymoon cottage. It just so happens Mr. LaMore has gone home to Canada for the next few months. You can use his place till you've put up one of your own." He led her down one of the narrow trails crisscrossing the small clearing. Jacob followed close behind. Soon after they passed the Clarke's place, they arrived at a tiny log structure set against the forest.

When Uncle Will swung open the rough-hewn door, a musty odor issued forth. Determined not to enter, Elizabeth drew away, only to encounter Jacob, who scooped her up in his arms.

"Put me down!"

"Not till I've carried my bride over the threshold!" Stepping into the dim cabin, Jacob came face to face with the greatest challenge of his life—convincing his new wife to spend even one night in a place featuring cobwebs for curtains, and nothing but a cot, table, and three-legged stool for furniture.

"Put me down! I'm going back to the boat!" Elizabeth protested again, thrashing so hard Jacob nearly dropped her before setting her on her feet.

"Surely you don't mean to leave so soon after coming all this way," Will countered, his wide form filling the doorway. "You haven't even given Riverton a chance!"

Elizabeth set her hands on her hips, and faced Will squarely. "Nor do I intend to. This isn't the town you bragged about. This is nothing but a forest! Now let me pass!"

In the distance, a steam whistle blew. Uncle Will's gray-brown beard and shaggy mustache parted in a toothy grin. "That's the *Governor Marcy* pulling away from the dock. I guess you'll be staying after all."

"Oh!" Elizabeth cried, so frustrated she wanted to pound her balled fists against the man's broad chest.

Jacob came alongside her, taking her hands in his. "I know this place isn't quite as fancy as you expected, but it's a roof over our heads."

"And it's got two six-paned windows with glass in them," Will pointed out. "Not every cabin has genuine glass. Besides that, the walls are chinked tight. And look here." He stepped to the back, near the open hearth. "There's even a bucket to carry your drinking water, and a crane to hold your cooking pot." He swung the iron arm back and forth, disturbing a spider that took off up the chimney.

Resigned to one night in the place, Elizabeth scraped her toe across the needle-strewn puncheon floor, sending two ants scurrying. "This place is filthy," she said in disgust.

"We can fix that," Will said, stepping outdoors.

Elizabeth looked at Jacob inquiringly.

He shrugged. Diverting his thoughts from serious apprehensions about Riverton, he took advantage of the moment to press a kiss against his wife's neck, still redolent with the fragrance of lilac-scented toilet water.

"Not now," she protested. "The moment hardly calls for affection."

Regardless, Jacob bent to kiss her, but the sound of a mosquito's buzz cut the affection short. He brushed the pest out of his wife's shiny, dark hair, then killed it with a clap of his hands. "We'll have to remember to keep the door shut," he commented.

Uncle Will returned with a pine bough and presented it to Elizabeth. "Your broom. While you're sweeping up, Jacob and I will fetch your trunk."

Alone in the cabin, Elizabeth wanted to cry, but tears would do no good. With her makeshift broom, she cleared needles and grit from the floor, and cobwebs from the corners and windows. When she swept the debris out the door, she noticed that kindling and firewood stood ready in a neat stack beside the house. At least she would have fuel for a cooking fire.

The men delivered her trunk and two firkins of provisions purchased in Detroit, then set off to fetch Jacob's belongings. In their absence, she eagerly opened her trunk and lifted out the very first item on top—the leather case of medical supplies her father, a physician in Brockport, had helped her prepare. Fond memories of accompanying him on his rounds and assisting in his office made her more eager than ever to depart this Michigan wilderness. Until she could return to her hometown, the sense of satisfaction and contentment she had derived from helping patients would be absent from her life.

Setting the medical kit aside, she focused again on the problem of making the cabin livable for one day. Taking out her linen tablecloth, she folded it in half and draped it over the crude table. The smooth, white fabric hung to the floor on all sides, hiding the ugly legs.

The pine needle mattress required attention next. Carrying it outdoors, she swatted the dust from its ticking, replaced it on the rope bed, and made it up with the sheet she had embroidered in yellow and blue flowers. She wondered what this night in the Saginaw wilderness would be like, snuggled beside Jacob in a bed obviously meant for one. The thought was interrupted when the men returned with Jacob's trunk and valise, and Elizabeth detected a hint of displeasure in the set of her husband's jaw.

Uncle Will set down his end of the heavy load and wiped his shirt sleeve across his damp, dirt-streaked forehead. "I'll leave so you two can finish settling in. If you need anything, I'll be at the blockhouse." Pine needles crunched beneath his feet as he disappeared down the trail.

Elizabeth opened her mouth to tell Jacob she would stay no more than this one night in Riverton, but closed it without a word when he suddenly slammed the door shut.

Unable to conceal the anger that had been brewing within, Jacob gave his valise a kick, sending it skidding across the floor. "Paper town!" he said with pure contempt.

8

"Beg your pardon?"

Jacob paced the room, head down, hands in pockets. He couldn't remember a time when he'd been as provoked as he was right now. Picking up his valise, he dumped its entire contents onto the bed and began pawing through the documents, searching for the map of Riverton his uncle had sent him several months ago. He found the tightly rolled drawing beneath the deed to his piece of "prime property" and opened it up on the table.

Tapping his finger on a square in the center of the chart, he told Elizabeth, "There it is. Our lot. The one Uncle Will *guaranteed* was right in the middle of town. Far as I can tell, the only thing it's in the middle of is a thick pine forest." He suddenly let go of the map and it snapped shut as he resumed his pacing. "I wish you could have heard Uncle Will when we got to the top of the riverbank with my trunk. We set it down for a rest, and he pointed off to the east. 'Jacob, don't you see it?' he said. 'The white clapboard houses and parks where the children play on swings and teeter-totters? A church and a schoolhouse stand right over there, on Center Avenue.'" Jacob moved his head from side to side. "The clapboard on all those houses is still growing in those pines!" He walked to one of the walls, studied it a moment, then gave it a whack with his fist. A clump of mud chink dropped to the floor.

Elizabeth swooped to retrieve it, tucking it back into its hole between the logs. In all the time Jacob had been courting her, she'd never seen him use force against anything. Plainly, he was a different man now that his righteous indignation was aroused.

Her own anger making her bold, she said, "Jacob, we can't let Uncle Will do this to us! I'm going to the block-

9

house this instant and tell him he's got to give back the money you paid him for our lot and get us passage back East." She headed for the door.

Jacob caught her by the wrist. "No, Elizabeth. I'll do it. I got us into this predicament. I'll get us out. Uncle Will won't cotton to a demand of money coming from you. He'll say you're just a silly young woman not willing to give this place a chance."

"And neither do I intend to!" she asserted, twisting away. But Jacob held firm, catching both her hands up in his, forcing her to face him.

Gazing into her snapping brown eyes, he spoke quietly. "Elizabeth, my love, it grieves me to see you upset." He pressed a kiss against her fingers and another on her forehead.

Jacob's tenderness, and the pleading look in his blue-as-the-bay eyes tempered Elizabeth's outrage. She couldn't keep from smiling just a little at her own weakness where her handsome new husband was concerned.

"That's better. I'll go see Uncle Will. But first, I'll fetch you some water so you can wash and start supper."

In Jacob's absence, Elizabeth brought in kindling. Reluctant to borrow hot coals from neighbors she hardly knew, she twirled two sticks together, wondering how long it would take her to light a fire using this primitive method, and how she would manage to prepare anything edible in such uncivilized circumstances. She had about given up on her effort when a voice sounded outside the closed cabin door.

"Mrs. Morgan? It's Clara Langton. I've brought hot coals for your fireplace, and some chowder for supper."

Elizabeth hastened to let her in. "You're exceedingly

10

kind, Mrs. Langton."

Ignoring the compliment, the slender woman went straight to the back of the cabin and set down her pans. Rearranging the dried moss and pine needles Elizabeth had set in the fireplace, Mrs. Langton turned out her hot coals and coaxed them into a small flame. Elizabeth crouched beside her, helping to set kindling in place as the fire grew. When there was no chance of it going out, Mrs. Langton rose and headed for the door, pausing only long enough to say, "You can find some berries for dessert down along the river."

"Thank you. I'll do that," Elizabeth hastily replied, but her words were cut off by the closing of the door. When the larger pieces of firewood had caught, she set the chowder on the crane to keep it warm, then rummaged in her trunk for a wooden bowl to hold berries. She was about to go in search of them when Jacob returned.

"There's a village well in the center of the clearing," he said, setting his bucket down near the hearth. "I see you already started a fire and set supper to simmering." He lifted the lid of the chowder pot. "Mm. Smells wonderful—like it's been cooking all day long. Makes me realize how hungry I am. I guess my talk with Uncle Will can wait until after we eat."

"Not so fast," Elizabeth said, taking him by the hand and leading him out the door. "While the two of you are having your discussion at the blockhouse, I'll go berry-picking."

Jacob helped his uncle roll the last of the barrels into the blockhouse, wiped the sweat from his brow with the back of his hand, and consulted his timepiece. Already, an

11

hour had passed since he'd come to discuss the prospect of leaving Riverton, but not a word had been spoken on the subject. Will had put Jacob to work right off, insisting talk could wait until they'd properly stored the supplies delivered by the *Governor Marcy*.

While Will leaned against a barrel and scraped out the bowl of his pipe, Jacob carefully approached his sticky problem, keenly aware that no purpose could be served by raising his uncle's ire. "I know how strongly you feel about Riverton, Uncle Will, but Elizabeth and I don't share your enthusiasm. We've talked it over, and we agree it's not for us. So if you'll just give us back the money for our lot, we'll catch the next boat out of here."

Will dropped his pipe into his shirt pocket and regarded Jacob contemplatively. "It's not quite that simple, Nephew."

"Why not?"

Without answering, Will pried open the barrel, removed a generous piece of salt pork, and tucked it into an empty flour sack. Putting an arm about Jacob's shoulder, he guided him out the door. "Polite or not, I'm inviting myself to supper with you and Elizabeth, and the three of us together will discuss this notion of yours to go back East."

In the cabin, Elizabeth sampled Mrs. Langton's chowder and said a prayer of thanks for this tasty dish that had been prepared for her. After nearly a month of eating in canal boat and hotel dining rooms, she was more skeptical than ever of her own cooking skills—almost non-existent except for the few lessons Hattie, her father's hired woman, had given her in the last two weeks before her wedding.

Elizabeth had just finished brewing the tea and setting the table for two when Jacob came through the door with

12

Will.

"Sorry to show up to dinner unexpected, Elizabeth," said Will, plunking his sack on the table so hard her delicate cups rattled in their saucers. "Ordinarily, I'd be too polite to invite myself in, but we've got some discussion ahead of us if you two are set on leaving." He opened his sack revealing the slab of salt pork. "Of course, I wouldn't come empty-handed."

Jacob slipped his arm about her waist. "Perhaps you can set a place for Uncle Will while I scare up enough seats for everyone."

Seeing no choice in the matter, Elizabeth nodded, then gathered up the sack of meat and handed it back to Will. "Dinner is already prepared. We won't be staying long enough to need this, but thanks for your thoughtfulness."

Reluctantly, Will took the sack. Opening his pocket-knife, he slit holes in the fabric near the top edge and hung the bag from a peg on the wall. "I'll just leave this here in case you decide to fry some meat up for breakfast."

While Elizabeth set out another place, ladled chowder into her green-painted china bowls, and poured tea, Jacob and Will arranged the stool and two trunks to serve as chairs.

At first, dinner table discussion consisted of bringing Will up to date on news from Brockport. Jacob was nearly finished with his bowl of chowder before he managed to bring the topic around to Riverton.

"When will the boat come through here again, Uncle Will?"

The bulk of his shoulders lifted. "Could be tomorrow. More likely than not, it'll be a week or more, though."

Elizabeth gasped. "A week? I can't possibly endure

this primitive existence for an entire week!"

Will chuckled. "I don't believe that for a minute, Elizabeth. Why, already you've got the place looking like you're all settled in." He indicated the made-up bed. "In any case, you've got no choice but to wait till the *Governor Marcy* gets loaded in Upper Saginaw and comes back downriver. No telling how long she'll tarry there to fill her hold."

"Oh." Elizabeth clamped her jaw shut to stifle the harsh rebuke on her tongue.

"I've got a mind to hike down to Upper Saginaw tomorrow and book passage," Jacob said. "Maybe Captain Winthrop will have some idea when he'll be returning to Detroit." His gaze locking on Will's, he added, "Of course, I'll need the cash money I gave you for the lot in order to pay for our tickets."

Will shifted in his seat. "Well, now, that puts a real snag in your brand new silk hose."

"You *do* have the money, don't you?" Elizabeth asked.

"Yes . . . and no. You see, it's not exactly in the form of hard cash right now."

"What, then?" Jacob inquired tersely.

Will drew an uneasy breath. "Remember all those barrels you helped me stack in the blockhouse?"

"You spent *our money* on supplies?" accused Elizabeth.

"Takes plenty of drygoods to weather the winter up here in the Saginaw Valley," Will explained.

"But it's not even the middle of summer yet!" Jacob noted. A new thought came to him. "Why don't you just sell off enough of those supplies to give us back our money?"

"Yes," Elizabeth agreed. "They're partly ours anyway,

14

bought with our investment, as they were."

Will put up his hands, his relentless good humor faultering. "Whoa. There are only two hitches in your line of thinking, young lady. First off, folks in these parts don't have cash money to buy the supplies. They get along day to day mostly by hard work, barter, and bull-headed determination. Second, the money you paid me for land was *mine*. You have no ownership in what it bought."

Elizabeth's cheeks burned with the anger she held in check by sheer will. "That might be so if the land you'd sold us was truly what you'd said. But you duped us! You told us we were buying a village lot. Instead, we were buying nothing but a piece of wilderness! Jacob and I have a rightful claim to a share of the goods in your warehouse, and somehow, some way, we'll convince Captain Winthrop to take them in trade for passage to Detroit." She rose. "I think it would be best for you to leave."

"Easy, now, Elizabeth," Uncle Will stalled. "No point in—"

"Please go!" she repeated, unmoved.

Will headed for the door, and Jacob could see by the set of his uncle's jaw that there would be no swaying him on this issue. Like it or not, he and Elizabeth were stranded in this wilderness for now. The best they could do would be to learn to get along while he searched for a way out.

He needed to think, to sort through some possibilities. His appetite spoiled, he rose from the table. "I'm going for a walk," he quietly told Elizabeth.

Still flushed with rage, she addressed him sharply. "That's right. Chase after him. But don't you *dare* apologize for me. I'm not one bit sorry for what I said. But I sure am sorry I ever let you bring me to this place!"

15

Her words augmenting his despair, he somberly replied, "I'm sorry, too, Elizabeth."

Head down, shoulders drooping, he disappeared out the door. The moment it closed behind him, Elizabeth realized she shouldn't have spoken so harshly to him, but her anger was too fresh for an apology. She slumped onto her stool, one thought dominating all others, that she would never know happiness again until she had left this rough, raw, wild, new state of Michigan.

CHAPTER

2

Jacob walked alone along the riverbank, unable to think of anything but Elizabeth. Her words echoed in his mind again and again. *I sure am sorry I ever let you bring me to this place.* He loved her so much, he'd missed being with her the very moment he'd left the cabin, but he couldn't go back to her until he'd sorted out his problems.

For nearly a year, they'd planned to move to the Saginaw Valley, never anticipating the hardships that lay in store. He wanted to knock his uncle silly for telling him such bold-faced lies about Riverton. At the same time, he knew he couldn't survive a week—or even two days—without his uncle's help. Angry or not, he couldn't afford to alienate the only man he knew between here and York State. Will could teach him the pioneering skills he so desperately needed in this raw, unhewn land—this wild country which was holding him hostage for the time being.

And freeing himself and Elizabeth from the Saginaw Valley would allow him to rekindle the happiness they had known until this sorry day. Kneeling in the grass on the riverbank, he bowed his head. "Dear heavenly Father, please be with me and guide me in the path that leads to better times. In Jesus' name, Amen."

Getting to his feet, he wandered toward the blockhouse. Dusk was falling, and lantern light spilled from the open door onto the pier, beckoning to him, as if in answer to his prayer.

Elizabeth had been in bed for hours, sleeping fitfully to the lullaby of howling wolves and hooting owls, when Jacob quietly entered the cabin and doused his lantern. She listened to him undressing, anticipating the moment when he crawled in bed beside her and wrapped his arms about her, snuggling close against her back. His embrace rekindled the sense of security she had been longing for since his departure, and she tried to turn toward him to tell him so, but his hold tightened, preventing her.

"Rest easy, my darling," he whispered in her ear. "I love you."

"And I love you, Jacob. I'm sorry for the way I spoke to you." She caressed the arms that held her fast.

"You're forgiven," he replied, kissing her hair.

The comfort of his touch and her weariness from travel soon caused her to fall fast asleep. When she finally awoke, it was morning and she was alone again. Dressing quickly, she set off to look for her husband at the blockhouse, her feet moving in rhythm to the distant sound of axes against standing timber. The moist air was redolent with pine, and hung in a fog over the river and blockhouse. Its door stood open, and she stepped inside a storage room that lay in semi-darkness.

"Jacob? Uncle Will?" she called, looking among the barrels and kegs that lined the walls, but the only answer was the fluttering of wings. A moment later, a bat swooped down from the rafters and out the door.

Supressing a squeal, she exited quickly, following a trail toward the chopping noise. In the midst of the towering trees, she discovered her husband and his uncle swinging axes in turn against a pine near the river. Sensing the danger of stepping too near, she watched them from a distance. Even so, the earth quivered beneath her feet when the trunk hit the ground.

In the eerie silence following the crash, she called out. "Jacob! I've been looking for you! Are you coming home for breakfast?"

A wide smile spread across his face when he saw her, then faded when Will spoke to him in words she couldn't hear. Together, they strode toward her.

Jacob took her hands in his and brushed her forehead with a kiss. "Good morning, my darling. I ate with Uncle Will a couple of hours ago. I couldn't bear to wake you. I wanted to get an early start clearing our lot."

"But—" Before she could ask why he would bother, when they would soon be leaving Riverton, Will interrupted.

"It's dangerous here while we're working, Elizabeth. I'd hate to see you get hurt. You'd best keep your distance for a month or two."

Warmth flooded her face. She wrenched her hands free from Jacob as she targeted him with her questions. "A month or two? What about passage home?"

He glanced at his uncle, then regarded her solemnly. "We need to find a buyer for our lot. We'll get more money for it if it's been cleared."

Elizabeth stood her ground. "I want to go back to Brockport! I can't possibly stay here for a month or two. Not even for a week!"

Jacob's gut wrenched with guilt. "I want to go back to Brockport, too, Elizabeth. Believe me, I've been over it and over it with Uncle Will. This is our best alternative."

Speechless with anger, she strode away.

Uncle Will called after her. "Elizabeth, you ought to pay Mrs. Clarke a call. It'll help pass the time till Jacob comes home for his midday meal."

Ignoring the suggestion, she went straight to her cabin. An hour later, when an attempt at cooking herself breakfast produced corn cakes too burnt for human consumption, she gave up in frustration, ate a cup of the blueberries she had picked the night before, and headed for the Clarke's cabin.

A latchstring hung outside the door bearing the wooden cross, and Elizabeth knew it was a pioneer tradition for callers to let themselves in, but she knocked instead.

Mrs. Clarke soon greeted her with a welcoming smile that lifted her spirits. "Do come in, Mrs. Morgan. I'll put on some water for tea." She indicated one of the two chairs at the oblong pine table, and Elizabeth sat while the older woman added wood to her fire. "How was your first night in Riverton?" she asked as she poured water into her kettle and swung it over the flames.

"It wasn't at all what I expected," Elizabeth said frankly.

Settling into the other chair, Mrs. Clarke chuckled. "The wolves kept me awake for an entire week afore I grew accustomed to them. Soon, you won't even notice." A thoughtful moment lapsed before she continued. "I remember well when Ben and I first arrived two years ago. We came on a mission to the Chippewa village—that's just down the river a piece. I was sure the Lord couldn't possibly intend for us to stay in such a dreadful place." Eyes twinkling, she added, "Since then, I've learned that sometimes the Lord puts us where He wants us, then He finds ways of keeping us there, in spite of ourselves!"

"I can't imagine any good reason for the Lord to want me here," Elizabeth said glumly. "My father could certainly use my help back home."

"Oh?" Mrs. Clarke's forehead wrinkled.

"He's a medical doctor. I helped him with his patients until Jacob and I married and left Brockport a month ago."

Mrs. Clarke checked the kettle of water, took teacups and a teapot from her shelf, then sat again. "The only medicine in these parts is what's being practiced by the Chippewa Medicine Man. He's got a fine remedy for snake bites, but he can't help his people when they're struck with the white man's diseases." A thoughtful moment lapsed, then Mrs. Clarke said, "I hear the water boiling. While I set the tea to steeping, why don't you tell me about your family? You've mentioned your father, but not your mother. Have you any brothers or sisters back in Brockport? That's a canal town, isn't it?"

Elizabeth spoke fondly of her mother, who had died fifteen years ago, and described her upbringing by her Aunt Sallie, who had suddenly and mysteriously disappeared when Elizabeth was thirteen. In turn, Mrs. Clarke described her own children and grandchildren, the pain of separation, and the joy in working for the Lord.

They had been sipping tea for an hour or more when, without warning, a young Indian woman clutching a blanket-wrapped bundle burst into the cabin. Elizabeth jumped up, spilling the last of her tea as she backed away.

"It's all right, Mrs. Morgan," the older woman assured her. "This is Beloved-of-the-Forest, from the Chippewa village."

The Indian woman seemed oblivious to the introduction. Focusing on Mrs. Clarke, she carried on in lamenting tones in her native tongue. Then, she folded back a corner of the blanket. Inside lay an obviously dead infant.

Elizabeth gasped. "Pock marks! Smallpox!"

"Are you quite sure?" asked Mrs. Clarke.

"Positive!" Elizabeth insisted. "By this time, all her people have been exposed. How many live in the Indian village?"

"About a hundred," Mrs. Clarke said, "but Beloved's husband and several other men are off hunting and fishing. Only seventy-five or eighty would be there now. Why?"

"My father supplied me with smallpox vaccine. I have enough for both her village and ours. We should all be vaccinated as soon as possible. I can give her the vaccine right now, if she'll allow it."

Mrs. Clarke spoke in Chippewa to Beloved-of-the-Forest. The Indian responded with an emphatic shake of her head.

The conversation in Chippewa continued, then Mrs. Clarke translated for Elizabeth. "Beloved-of-the-Forest says only her father, the Chief, can decide whether the Chippewa should receive the white man's medicine for spotted fever. I'll go with her now, and my husband and I will explain it to him. If he agrees, I'll come back for you. How is the vaccine administered?"

"I scratch the arm enough to make it bleed, then I touch the wound with a thread that's been dipped in a serum containing the virus. The vaccination takes but a few seconds. Let me give it to you before you go. I'll fetch my supplies."

When Elizabeth had vaccinated Mrs. Clarke, she tucked her medical kit under her arm and set out to tell Jacob and

22

Will the sad news. As she hurried along the woodland trail, she prayed. "Thank you, Lord, for the vaccine Papa gave me before we left New York. Thank you, too, that there's enough to save the Riverton folks, and the Chippewas, too. Please be with Mrs. Clarke as she speaks to the Chief, and direct me as I give the vaccine to others. In Jesus' name, Amen."

She hurried faster toward the sound of axes, pausing several yards short of the tree where Jacob and his uncle were working.

"Jacob! Uncle Will!" she shouted above the chopping noise. When they had put down their axes, she lifted her skirt and ran to them.

Will regarded her sternly. "I thought I told you to keep clear of here."

Jacob ignored his uncle. "What is it, Elizabeth? Is someone hurt?" He indicated the medical kit she was holding.

She shook her head. "There's an outbreak of smallpox among the Chippewa." To Will, she said, "This is the vaccine Papa gave me."

"Not smallpox," Will said, his tone full of dread.

Jacob's head moved slowly from side to side. "At least we can be thankful your father had foresight enough to send the serum along with us. Maybe nobody in Riverton will be affected, if you administer it right away. Too bad about the Chippewa, though."

"Mrs. Clarke has gone to the Chippewa village to ask permission from the Chief for me to make his people safe from the disease," Elizabeth explained. Focusing on Will, she continued. "But while I'm waiting to hear, I could take care of you and the Riverton folks."

He nodded. "Come with me to the blockhouse. I'll ring the bell to gather everybody 'round."

Within minutes the Farrells, Langtons, Sayers, and a family Elizabeth hadn't seen before, gathered together. A gruff-looking man slipped a bottle from his pocket and took a nip, then wiped the back of his hand across his matted mustache and stepped up to Will.

"This had better be import'nt, Morgan," the man warned, his speech slurred. "I got better things t'do 'n come runnin' 'cause you rung the bell."

A meek and timid woman, whom Elizabeth assumed to be his wife, shrank back, her eyes downcast. A toddling son clung to her skirt, while a young puppy no more than two months old frolicked at their feet.

A hush fell over the gathering as Will addressed the fellow boldly. "It's important, Tyler. Unless you want a case of the smallpox."

Mrs. Farrell gasped. Mrs. Sayer and Mrs. Langton whispered to one another.

Captain Langton, a trim, wiry fellow sporting a commodore's cap, spoke up. "Who's got the pox?"

Elizabeth stepped forward to answer. "Beloved-of-the-Forest's baby died of smallpox this morning."

Will spoke again. "We're mighty lucky my nephew and his new wife arrived here when they did. Elizabeth's father is a doctor back East. He gave her enough supplies to vaccinate us all."

Tyler made a grunting sound. "I ain't never been to no doctor of med-cin, and I sure won't let no female imitator touch me, neither!" On wobbly legs, he turned to leave.

Will shouted after him. "You're a fool, Tyler!"

Tyler swung around, fists balled. "What's 'at?"

"I said you're nothing but a drunk, lazy fool!"

Tyler swung wildly. Will ducked the punch, then wrestled the man to the ground, twisting his arms behind him and straddling his backside. "I know you went to the Chippewa camp to trade firewater for that new pup of yours. Your family's exposed. At least let your wife and son take the vaccination."

"No!" Tyler argued, trying to wrench free.

Will tightened his grip. Captain Langton knelt beside them and pulled the bottle from Tyler's back pocket. Uncapping it, he threatened to pour its contents onto the ground right in front of Tyler's face. "What do you say now, Zeb Tyler?"

After a moment's struggle, he went limp. "All right. The wife 'n boy. But keep that imposter away from me."

Tyler slunk off to indulge in his bottle as Elizabeth administered the vaccinations. Mrs. Tyler and her son were last in line. By the time Elizabeth came to them, Zeb was nowhere in sight.

Elizabeth rolled up Mrs. Tyler's tattered sleeve, and couldn't help noticing a prominent bruise on the woman's arm. She was certain by the way Mrs. Tyler refused to meet her gaze, that her husband had been the cause.

When Elizabeth had finished vaccinating the Tyler boy, his mother spoke quietly. "I'm mighty thankful to ya for this, Mrs. Morgan. I 'pologize for what my husband said 'bout ya." She pushed a loose strand of straight brown hair back toward her tangled bun.

Elizabeth accepted the apology with a nod. "If there's any way I can help you, call on me, won't you?"

Her gaze shifted downward. "I . . . thank ya, ma'am." Taking her little boy by the hand, she started up the riverbank stairs, the puppy trailing close behind. A piece of Elizabeth's heart went with them, and a sense of helplessness and frustration set in. Jacob must have guessed her mood, for he put a consoling hand on her shoulder.

"You've done all you can for the Tylers, for now," he said. Elizabeth was still pondering the situation when Jacob pointed to the top of the riverbank. "Look. Mrs. Clarke is back."

Together, they hurried to the top of the steps. The older woman was short of breath, but spoke rapidly.

"The Chief has accepted your offer of the vaccination. I'll take you to him now." As she led Elizabeth and Jacob along a narrow riverside trail, she told of the work she and her husband had been doing among the Chippewa. "We've taught them how to speak English—in a very elementary way, mind you—and how to better cultivate their vegetable gardens. And of course, we've shared the gospel with them. So far none of the Chippewa have accepted Christ, but we're not about to give up!"

Several minutes later, they entered a village comprised of bark-covered huts. Beside one of the dome-shaped wigwams, several dogs lay in the dirt, and growled as they passed by.

Elizabeth linked her arm with Jacob's. "They surely don't look like family pets. They look like wolves, almost."

"They're a crossbreed," Mrs. Clarke explained. "Brother-of-the-Wolf raises them. They rarely make pets of their animals, like we do. They use them as a source of food, or to pull a sledge in the wintertime."

"You can't mean they actually *eat* those dogs," Elizabeth said.

"I'm afraid it's so," Mrs. Clarke replied. A minute later, she led Elizabeth and Jacob to the narrow end of a long, low building at the center of the village. "Ben and the Chief are here, in the council lodge. They're expecting us." She drew back the animal skin that served as a door.

Elizabeth had to stoop to enter. Inside, shafts of light streamed from the smoke holes overhead. At the far end, the figures of Reverend Clarke and the Chief were barely visible. Mrs. Clarke approached the men, speaking to the Chief in his own language.

The Chief nodded, and replied in a somber tone. Mrs. Clarke translated for Elizabeth and Jacob. "My medicine man has great power, but he cannot stop the spotted fever. Soon, my people will gather here. Thank you for coming to help us."

As if by magic, the villagers quietly gathered at the council house. Elizabeth noted the unclad children, and how their mothers greased and carefully plaited their own ebony hair. The men were robust and broad featured. Many of them were taller than Jacob.

Though Elizabeth understood that breech cloths, moccasins, and arm bands were their normal dress, she was unaccustomed to such scantily clad men, and tried not to stare at the coppery skin and well-defined muscles.

One brave in particular stood out, his chest very broad, his arms and legs unusually rugged. When he had received his vaccination and exited the lodge, Elizabeth spoke of him to Mrs. Clarke. "I've never seen such strength in a man."

"He's the best hunter of the village—Brother-of-the-Wolf—the one who raises the dogs," Mrs. Clarke explained.

Elizabeth nodded, then pushed thoughts of the hunter

aside as she continued to administer the vaccination. The last to come to her was Beloved-of-the-Forest, who spoke to her through Mrs. Clarke.

"Thank you, daughter of white medicine man. Though it is too late for my child, the kindness you have shown today will save many of my people." She bowed her head and left on quiet moccasins.

"She seems to have changed her attitude about the serum since this morning," Elizabeth commented to Mrs. Clarke.

"When I came with her to her father, he impressed upon her how generous your offer was, and how important the vaccinations were. He told her that, in times past, whole tribes had been wiped out by smallpox. He said this village could be destroyed in a matter of days if not for your help."

"Thank God for the Chief's wisdom," Elizabeth replied reverently.

Later that evening, while Elizabeth was sitting on the cot, brushing out her hair, she thought back on all that had happened her first full day in Riverton. A great sense of satisfaction came over her, knowing the number of people she had helped. Begrudgingly, she admitted to herself that she felt more useful here today, than in all the years she had worked alongside her father in Brockport.

Jacob sat down beside her, his expression pensive. "Elizabeth, do you know what I was just thinking?"

She put away her brush and gazed into his blue-as-heaven eyes. "That you love me and you're glad you married me?" She offered a teasing smile.

He couldn't help grinning in return. "You *know* that's true. I was thinking of something else, too." He wrapped his arm about her shoulders and pulled her close. "I was thinking that if you hadn't been here with the vaccine, this whole town could have been wiped out almost before it got started."

His words brought to mind those spoken by Mrs. Clarke earlier that day. *. . . sometimes, the Lord puts us where He wants us, then He finds ways of keeping us there, in spite of ourselves!*

Outside, a wolf howled, and somewhere in the immediate vicinity, a mosquito buzzed. How she longed for the civilized sounds of Brockport—of carriage wheels against bricks on Monroe Avenue where she had grown up, and barges tooting warnings of their approach on the Erie Canal. But she was hundreds of miles from there, with no hope of returning anytime soon.

"Jacob," she spoke thoughtfully, "do you think that's why the Lord brought us here? To save Riverton, and the Chippewa village?"

He gazed into the eyes of the woman he had fallen in love with from the first moment of their meeting long ago. She was growing more beautiful with each passing day, not only on the outside, but within, and his love for her was increasing daily, as well. He prayed he could make her as happy here, in Riverton, as she was making him.

His mind raced through his own reasons for bringing her to Michigan—to make a good investment for their future, to prove himself a success. He thought, too, of the new dream his uncle had shared with him last night—of starting a bank together. He prayed for God's guidance in every decision.

"Elizabeth, darling, I don't honestly know if the Lord brought us here to save people from smallpox, or for some other reason, but I'm glad we were here to help." Kissing her briefly on the cheek, he said, "I don't know about you, but this has been one tiring day for me. I'm ready to turn in." He rotated his shoulders, trying to loosen muscles grown tight from swinging an ax, and couldn't help wincing at the soreness setting in.

Elizabeth knew without asking, why he looked so chagrined. "You've overdone. Let me rub on some liniment."

He took off his shirt, pulled back the sheet, and lay on the bed face down. As she worked the balm into his shoulders, he recalled the bulky muscles on the men he'd seen at the Chippewa village. "Those Indian braves sure look like strong fellows, don't they," he mused.

Elizabeth chuckled softly. "They'd give even the toughest New York farm boys a real time of it in arm wrestling."

"Uncle Will says he's never seen anybody who can hunt and fish like they can. Did you know, for a Spanish quarter, you can buy a fish from the Chippewa that's big enough to feed a family of nine?"

She laughed. "It'll be a good long while before we'll have need of a fish that big."

"I suppose you're right," he commented, allowing his eyes to close. The relaxing effect of Elizabeth's ministrations soon brought deep slumber.

He had no idea how long he'd been asleep when he awoke with a start to raucous yells, and a fierce pounding on the door. The cabin lay in darkness except for a slice of moonlight. He tried to think what to do, then scrambled out of bed and began shoving his trunk across the floor toward the door.

"Jacob, what is it?" Elizabeth's voice was full of fear, and in the candescent light, he could see her starting to get up.

"Stay put, Elizabeth!" he ordered, shoving her trunk up against his.

The assaults on the door grew louder, and Jacob heard its wooden plank crack. He grabbed a stick of firewood and positioned himself between the table and the cot.

With one mighty bang, the door ripped from its hinges and the marauder fell inside, sprawled across the two trunks. In the sliver of moonlight, Jacob recognized their intruder.

CHAPTER

3

"Brother-of-the-Wolf! Get out!" Jacob ordered.

The Chippewa righted himself, crouched low, and pulled out a hunting knife. Mumbling unintelligibly, he brandished the weapon in Jacob's direction.

"You're drunk! Go home!" Jacob insisted.

The Indian lunged at him. Jacob sidestepped the stabbing blade, then upended the table to use as a shield. "Get out!" he shouted again.

Brother-of-the-Wolf lunged forward, embedding his knife in the table. Enraged, he wrenched the table from Jacob and sent it crashing against the cabin wall. Turning on Jacob once more, he swung at him with his bare fist.

Jacob ducked the blow, then grabbed the stool for protection. Brother-of-the-Wolf ripped the stool from his grasp, then lifted Jacob by his nightshirt and slammed him against the wall. Dazed by the blow to his head, Jacob slumped to the floor, his mind in a muddle.

Elizabeth watched in horror as Brother-of-the-Wolf tore into one of the trunks. Fistful by fistful, he flung the contents across the cabin.

Panicked, she scrambled off the bed and grabbed her iron frying pan. As her bone china dishes crashed against the cabin wall, she tip-toed around behind him.

Coming to his senses, Jacob picked up a broken table leg and hurled it at Brother-of-the-Wolf, hitting him aside the head. He fell unconscious, landing on the floor with a thud.

Elizabeth's knees grew weak. The iron frying pan slipped from her hand. Trembling, she sagged to the floor, her stomach churning from fright.

Jacob picked her up and set her on the bed. He held her tight. "It's all over, my darling. You're safe, now."

She began to cry. "Why did he do this to us? We tried to help him. I don't understand!"

"Easy, darling. Calm down." Jacob kissed her cheek, her forehead, her nose, then placed his mouth over hers, finally quieting her sobs. When the kiss ended, he said, "Uncle Will cautioned me about Indians who get into drink. 'Makes them more cussed than a hungry Michigan bear,' he said. I laughed at the time, but now I know to take his warning to heart."

Elizabeth blew her nose into a handkerchief, then lay her head against Jacob's shoulder. "I still don't understand why Brother-of-the-Wolf broke into our cabin."

Before Jacob could speculate on the reason, a lantern light appeared at the door. Reverend Clarke, clad in nightcap and robe, paused at the threshold. "Lord, have mercy. Are you folks hurt?" He held his lantern high to survey the wreckage.

"We're all right," Jacob answered, despite the headache that was now coming on with a vengeance.

China crunched beneath Ben Clarke's slippers as he climbed past the broken door. Lowering his light, he stooped down beside Brother-of-the-Wolf, his nose wrinkling. "Whiskey. I was afraid of this. He turns savage when he's under the influence of strong drink. Then he goes in search of more." The pastor's bulky form rising, he turned to Elizabeth. "He knew you had medical supplies. He probably assumed he'd find more whiskey here."

"Whiskey?" Elizabeth asked incredulously. "I very nearly brought whiskey, but Papa had none to spare, so we came without. Now, our cabin is in ruins, all for the lack of whiskey!" Giddy from the release of tension, she began to chuckle. Her chuckles grew to laughter, and soon, Jacob and Reverend Clarke joined in.

Their moment of lightheartedness was coming to an end when Captain Langton showed up. "I must be thicker than I thought," he concluded, scratching his sideburn, "but I don't see anything funny here. Just one whale of a mess. I'm going to get Clara. She'll help set things right in no time."

Brother-of-the-Wolf groaned, and Reverend Clarke knelt beside him. Speaking in Chippewa, he slapped the brave gently on the cheeks, but couldn't rouse him. "Jacob, if you can help, I'll take this slumbering piece of humanity to my cabin for the night. Then you folks can tidy up and get some rest."

"My pleasure," Jacob said.

By the time they had hauled the Indian out, Mrs. Langton had come with a cornbroom and dust pan. While she swept up broken china, Elizabeth put the trunks in order again, thankful that her medical kit was still intact.

Sometime in the wee hours of the morning, Jacob finished hanging a sheet as a temporary door and crawled in bed beside Elizabeth. Though he seemed to have no difficulty falling asleep, Elizabeth lay awake for a long time wondering when and how they would make their departure for the East. All the satisfaction she had felt at helping the Indians was now dashed, knowing she could never feel safe as long as she lived here.

She raised the subject of leaving Michigan over a breakfast of salt pork and golden brown corncakes. Until Jacob could repair the leg of their table, they were reduced to balancing their plates—the only two not broken by Brother-of-the-Wolf—on their laps. Elizabeth set hers aside on the shelf in order to better concentrate on what she was about to say.

"Jacob, we've got to find a way out of here."

Swallowing the last of his syrup-soaked corn cake, he lay his fork down and focused on Elizabeth, her brown eyes dark with concern. "I know, my darling. I just don't know quite how we're going to do it. We have only a few silver dollars to our names. Passage here was more expensive than I had expected, being held over in Detroit for so long as we were. The supplies we bought there were costly, too."

"Let's go to Upper Saginaw. Maybe we can find someone there to buy our share of the supplies in Uncle Will's blockhouse—"

"Elizabeth," Jacob cut in, a wrinkle of concern deepening in his forehead, "you heard what Uncle Will said. We can claim no ownership in any part of his supplies."

She pressed her lips together to contain the arguments on the tip of her tongue. When her anger had subsided, she calmly suggested, "Then perhaps you could get a job. There's bound to be someone there with a need for a hired hand, and you're a mighty hard worker."

Inwardly, Jacob bridled at the thought of hiring himself out. Working on his own piece of land in the Saginaw

Valley was one thing. Toiling as a day laborer for paltry wages was something else—especially for a man who'd been accustomed to earning a good salary in his father's bank.

But Elizabeth's happiness was at stake, and he couldn't blame her for wanting to get out of Riverton after last night's scare. "Upper Saginaw is a long hike from here— four miles, at least. You'd better stay here."

"I wouldn't dream of it!"

From the set of her jaw, he knew there would be no dissuading her. "Then put on your walking shoes, lady. If we're going, we'd best get on our way. But remember what Uncle Will said. Most people trade by barter. Even if I find work, I probably won't find anyone paying cash money for it."

"Maybe Captain Winthrop will hire you on, and you could work off our passage en route." When Jacob's brow rose skeptically, she said, "Just promise me you'll ask. That's all I want."

He put his plate aside and took her in his arms. His heart was so full of love for his intelligent, yet innocent wife, he lifted her off her feet, spun around, then set her down and kissed her soundly. "You know I can't refuse you, my darling."

Her heart soaring, she kissed him back, and as the kiss threatened to become more, she couldn't help thinking how much she loved being in his arms, and how truly happy she would be once their embraces were taking place on York State soil.

Reluctantly, she broke off the kiss. "Like you said, we'd best get on our way. I'll pack us a lunch."

"And I'll fetch some fresh water."

While Jacob went to the well, Elizabeth carefully wrapped leftover corncakes in a linen napkin and put on her sturdy leather shoes. As they walked out of the makeshift door, Jacob said, "I feel really strange, leaving the cabin with only a flimsy sheet for a door." Gazing at the cloudless, blue sky, he added, "I suppose repair of the wooden one can wait a day, since it doesn't look like rain."

Elizabeth took him by the hand and started down the trail. "Come on. There's time tomorrow to fix the door."

A minute later, they came to the Clarke's cabin. Mrs. Clarke was scrubbing laundry in a bucket out front. She paused to greet them. "Good morning, Mr. and Mrs. Morgan! I see you've recovered from last night. Brother-of-the-Wolf hasn't stirred. I'm afraid he'll be feeling the effects of his folly for some time."

"Hello, Mrs. Clarke," Elizabeth said cheerfully. "We're on our way to Upper Saginaw. We're going to see Captain Winthrop about passage back to Detroit."

"I'm sorry you've decided not to stay in Riverton," she said with meaning. "I suppose I can't blame you, after what happened last night." As she wrung out a towel and hung it on a branch to dry, she said, "There's a prairie full of rattle snakes between here and Upper Saginaw, Mrs. Morgan. Have you bound your legs with grass ropes so you won't get bit?"

Elizabeth shook her head. "I've never heard of such a thing."

Mrs. Clarke dried her hands on her apron. "Wait right here. I'll fetch mine and show you how to put them on." She returned moments later, and Elizabeth sat on a stump while Mrs. Clarke helped her with the protective covering. "Beloved-of-the-Forest taught me about the grass ropes,"

Mrs. Clarke said. "She's been helpful to me in many ways."

"Doesn't Jacob need grass ropes, too?" Elizabeth asked.

Mrs. Clarke shook her head. "His boots will prevent him from getting bit." To Jacob, she said, "But it would be a good idea for you to walk ahead of your wife, and pass a walking stick back and forth through the grass in front of you to scare the snakes from your path, just in case."

"Thanks for the advice, Mrs. Clarke. I'll remember."

Rising from the stump, Elizabeth said, "I'll be sure to return these to you as soon as we get back."

Mrs. Clarke nodded. "Have a pleasant sojourn!"

Setting off on the trail again, they had gone no farther than the steps leading to the blockhouse when they encountered Uncle Will.

"I was just coming to find you, Nephew. I heard you had some wolf trouble last night—the two-legged variety." He chortled.

Feeling uncomfortable with the comment, Jacob remained quiet until his uncle's laughter had subsided. "Elizabeth and I are on our way to Upper Saginaw to see Captain Winthrop about passage out of Riverton. We're heading home to Brockport as soon as we can make the arrangements."

Will frowned. "You're not going to let a little Indian trouble scare you away now, are you? I had you figured for a much tougher sort than that."

"It's Elizabeth's safety I'm concerned for," Jacob replied.

Irked by his uncle's attitude, and Jacob's readiness to blame her for the decision to leave, Elizabeth launched into Will. "You have no idea what it was like, having a stranger break your door down in the middle of the night, then start smashing nearly every piece of china you own. If you had any conscience at all, you'd give Jacob and me our share of your supplies and send us back to Brockport with your blessings!"

Will shifted from one foot to another, his complexion growing ruddy. "All right. You tell Captain Winthrop when you see him that you've got supplies equal to the price you paid for your land as barter for passage to Buffalo. He'll take you as far as Detroit, and work out the arrangements from there. But you're making a whale of a mistake leaving now, just when Riverton is about to prosper. In a couple of years, when I'm rich and you're back in Brockport no better off than the day you got married, I won't have you blaming me for not telling you to stay in Michigan!" He strode off.

Silent moments lapsed before Elizabeth spoke, highly aware of the vexed, hurt look on Jacob's face as he watched Will disappear down the trail into the village. "I didn't mean to get him so riled up." She slipped her hand in Jacob's.

He focused on Elizabeth, his heart pulled in two directions—how to be the protector and provider she needed, yet salvage some sense of satisfaction in the process. "He'll have plenty of time to calm down before we get back. Come on. We've got a long day ahead of us."

He took a route past their piece of Riverton property on his way to the Upper Saginaw trail. Though he'd only started to clear the plot, he could imagine a frame house rising amidst the trees, and children playing hide-and-seek among the white pines. He paused to pick up a stripped branch for a walking stick. Using it as a pointer, he said teasingly to Elizabeth, "Can't you see our white clapboard house with green shutters, smell the smoke rising from our chimney, and hear our children laughing and playing?"

She gave him a playful shove. "You're almost as full of foolish talk as your uncle! I wish I'd known it ran in the family before I married you."

Turning serious, he said, "Do you really?"

She gazed into the depths of his eyes, then smiled slyly. "I'd have married you anyway. I just wouldn't have believed everything I'd been told about Riverton. Now come on. The sooner we get to Upper Saginaw, the sooner we can get back to Brockport."

Following Jacob along a trail that had been worn down by many a moccasin, Elizabeth was pleased to leave the forest behind after a couple of miles, and enter the prairie. The tall grass was alive with the rattling of snakes. Though one of them attacked Jacob's walking stick, and another one tried to bite through her grass rope leggings, she came to no harm. About an hour after leaving Riverton, they paused at the edge of the prairie to eat their corncake lunch and sip from the flask of water Jacob carried. A few minutes later, they reached Upper Saginaw.

Elizabeth paused at the end of the main street, a few steps away from a general store. The bench out front looked inviting. "It's not much bigger than Riverton, but at least it has a drygoods." She read the sign above the shop. "Pierce's Mercantile."

"They've got a few things Riverton hasn't got, that's for certain," Jacob observed, indicating the businesses across the street. "The Western Hotel, the Saginaw Mill, and," pointing to the dock at the end of the street, he added, "the *Governor Marcy*."

"That looks like Captain Winthrop, going into the taproom of the hotel," Elizabeth said excitedly.

She started in that direction, but Jacob held her back. Pulling a coin from his pocket, he placed it in her palm and folded her fingers over it. "You know you'd have to wait for me in the parlor if you go over to the hotel. You might as well browse in the store. We both know how much you like to shop. Besides, you look like you could use a sweet about now. I'll be back for you in a while."

Reluctantly, Elizabeth accepted the coin. "I'll be praying for good news when you're done," she told Jacob as he started across the street. She waited until he had disappeared inside the hotel, then stepped into the general store.

A round-figured woman with a nose like a hawk's beak came from behind the counter to greet her. "Good afternoon! I don't believe I've seen you in these parts. I'm Olive Pierce. And you're . . . ?"

"Mrs. Jacob Morgan," Elizabeth told her.

"Then you're related to Will Morgan, in Riverton," the woman quickly concluded. "I'd heard tell his nephew and wife would be moving up there. I'll bet you arrived two days ago on the *Governor Marcy*. From York State, aren't you? Near Rochester?"

"Yes," Elizabeth replied, surprised to discover how quickly news traveled, even in these remote parts.

"Welcome to Upper Saginaw! Now, how can I be of service?"

"I'll need a few minutes to browse," she told the woman.

"Of course! Browse to your heart's content. No telling how long it can take a man to tend to his p's and q's." She nodded in the direction of the taproom, evidently referring to the pints and quarts served there.

"My husband doesn't take strong drink," Elizabeth quickly informed the woman. "He went to see someone about business."

"Of course," she said again, obviously unconvinced. "If there's anything I can help you with, just speak up."

"I will," Elizabeth promised, though her tolerance of the woman was quickly reaching its limit.

She hadn't browsed for long when she concluded that the selection of merchandise in Upper Saginaw was far more limited than in her hometown of Brockport, and far more expensive. Even the candy had reached premium prices, costing twice what she would have paid in York State. Begrudgingly, she took two peppermint sticks from the jar and laid them on the counter along with her coin.

"Are you sure that's all you need today, Mrs. Morgan? I have some attractive cotton broadcloth on sale." The brown paper sign showed the original price crossed out and a lower price written in.

"No, thank you, Mrs. Pierce," Elizabeth said, shoving the coin across the counter.

"Would you like me to wrap up the candy, or are you going to eat it?"

"I'll eat one now, and take the other wrapped," Elizabeth informed her. Mrs. Pierce counted her change and wrapped one of the candy sticks. Elizabeth scooped them up from the counter. "Good day, Mrs. Pierce." On her way out of the store, she paused to admire a walnut scroll rocking chair. It bore a very modest price, and the velvet seat and chair back cushions gave it a special appeal.

"Made locally of fine Michigan hardwood," Mrs. Pierce informed her. "Sit down. Try it out."

Despite the fact she would be leaving Michigan and had no use for such a chair, Elizabeth couldn't resist sitting in it to rest her tired legs. A minute later, she wondered if she would ever be able to get up. The chair was by far more comfortable than anything she'd sat on since leaving Brockport. She rocked back and forth, appreciating the action of the runners.

"I'll include delivery to Riverton at no extra charge, if you pay cash money for that rocker today," Mrs. Pierce said enticingly.

Elizabeth rocked back and forth a few more times, then reluctantly stood up. "Not today, thank you," she said.

As she headed for the door, a tall young Chippewa man entered, bringing the obvious odor of bear grease with him. Beloved-of-the-Forest followed close behind carrying several baskets—some of black ash and others of birch bark—on her arms.

"Beloved-of-the-Forest, how nice to see you," Elizabeth said.

"Greetings, Medicine Lady!" replied the young woman. She spoke to her companion in Chippewa, then again to Elizabeth. "Medicine Lady, my husband, Walks Tall."

"Pleased to meet you, Walks Tall," Elizabeth said.

The Chippewa nodded, his expression never changing from the stoic countenance universal among his tribe.

Mrs. Pierce came hustling over. "What do you want?" she demanded harshly of the Chippewas. "Speak up, or be on your way. I can't have you savages hanging around here, fouling the atmosphere for the rest of my customers."

Beloved-of-the-Forest went straight to the cotton fabrics, pointed to a bolt of solid red, and held out her arms laden with baskets. "Trade?"

"Ha!" Mrs. Pierce scoffed. "I have no need of baskets. Can't you see I have plenty of baskets?" She indicated the wickerware stacked in a corner—baskets looking far less substantial than Beloved-of-the-Forest's.

Mrs. Pierce continued. "If you want to trade here, bring me tanned deerskin, three hides for the bolt. Now off with you!" She gestured toward the door. When Beloved-of-the-Forest didn't move, Mrs. Pierce picked up her cornbroom and swatted the Indian woman's bare legs. "Go on, now! Shoo! Go back to where you came from!"

Walks Tall moved silently and swiftly out the door, Beloved-of-the-Forest one step behind.

Elizabeth picked up her skirt and hurried after them. "Beloved-of-the-Forest, Walks Tall, wait!"

The young Indian woman spoke in Chippewa to her husband, who went on without her, then she turned to Elizabeth.

"Beloved-of-the-Forest, I need a basket," Elizabeth said, pointing to the square one on the end of the Chippewa woman's arm.

The Indian woman shook her head. "Come. I have better one." Leading Elizabeth to the river where Walks Tall waited by their canoe, Beloved-of-the-Forest set her small baskets in the vessel and took out a larger one. "Cooking basket," she told Elizabeth.

"Cooking?"

Before Elizabeth could question the Indian further, Beloved-of-the-Forest waded knee-deep into the river, scooped water into the basket, and brought it ashore. To Elizabeth's amazement, the basket held the water without leaking a drop.

Beloved-of-the-Forest set the basket down and picked up a medium-sized rock. "Make fire. Heat many," she explained, meaning the rock. Then she set it in the water in the basket. "Cook."

"How much?" Elizabeth asked, taking the coins from her pocket to show Beloved-of-the-Forest.

Beloved-of-the-Forest shook her head. Dumping the water and rock from the basket, she said, "I tell you legend of basket. Old woman lives in moon, making basket. When finished, world will end. From time to time, the dog called by white man, Eclipse, comes and ruins her work. Then she starts over." Presenting the cooking basket to Elizabeth, Beloved-of-the-Forest said, "Gift for Medicine Lady."

"But—"

"Gift!" Beloved-of-the-Forest insisted.

Elizabeth accepted the basket. Realizing she would insult the woman by forcing payment on her, an idea flashed in her mind. She set the basket on the ground between them. "Thank you, Beloved-of-the-Forest. Now, you wait here, by your basket. Medicine Lady come right back."

As quickly as Elizabeth could, she hurried up the riverbank and into the store. Mrs. Pierce looked up from the counter where she was rearranging merchandise, and put on a smile. "Mrs. Morgan, you're back."

"I've decided to take you up on the sale of cotton piece goods," Elizabeth explained. Taking the bolt of red from the shelf, she laid it on the counter. "Five yards, please." She counted out exactly the right change to pay for the fabric at the sale price.

Mrs. Pierce reached for the bolt, then hesitated, a look

of suspicion in her small, gray eyes. Stepping out from behind the counter, she marched across the floor to the yard goods, ripped the brown paper "Sale" sign from its tack, and tore it in two. "The sale is over, Mrs. Morgan. I'll sell you three yards for that amount."

"Mrs. Pierce—" Elizabeth began to object, but the woman cut her off.

"Three yards! Or put some more money on the counter," she insisted.

Despite an intense urge to tell the shopkeeper off and stomp out, Elizabeth dug into her pocket, forced the corners of her mouth upward, and spoke sweetly as she lay additional coins on the counter. "That should do it for five yards, shouldn't it, Mrs. Pierce?"

The woman swept the coins into her hand, tossed them into a metal box behind the counter, and closed the lid with a clank. "So pleased serve to you, Mrs. Morgan," she said, unrolling the bolt and measuring from the tip of her nose to the end of her short arm.

"Excuse me, Mrs. Pierce, but I need a *full* five yards, no less, or the piece will do me no good. I'd suggest you use your measuring stick."

Reluctantly, Mrs. Pierce took the yardstick from its nail on the wall behind her and measured out an honest five yards. Folding it into a square, she slid it across the counter to Elizabeth. "There. Five yards of red broadcloth. Will there be anything else, Mrs. Morgan? Thread, perhaps?"

"Thanks for reminding me. Two spools should do, and a package of needles," she said. As the woman chose the items from the display nearby, Elizabeth again put the exact change on the counter. "Now, if you'll wrap it all up in brown paper and tie it with string, I'll be all set—except for a couple more peppermint sticks—wrapped separately, of course."

"Of course," said Mrs. Pierce somewhat sarcastically. She finished quickly, biting off the string with her teeth, then handing the parcels to Elizabeth. "That should do it for you, Mrs. Morgan."

Elizabeth took the parcels and hurried back to the river-bank where Beloved-of-the-Forest and Walks Tall were resting beneath the shade of an oak tree a few yards from their canoe. They quickly got to their feet when they saw her.

Elizabeth held out the parcels to Beloved-of-the-Forest. "Trade for basket."

"No," said the Chippewa firmly. "Basket is gift."

Finding a new angle, Elizabeth said, "Basket is gift from Beloved-of-the-Forest to Medicine Lady." Indicating the paper-wrapped packages, she continued. "These are gift from Medicine Lady to Beloved-of-the-Forest."

When the Chippewa woman folded her arms across her chest, Elizabeth set down the larger package and un-wrapped the candy canes, offering one to each of the Indians. "Gift. Please."

Following a nod from Walks Tall, they accepted the candy canes and immediately began to enjoy them.

Elizabeth knelt down, pulled the string off the larger parcel, and with care not to lose the thread and needles, began to unfold the red broadcloth. "For Beloved-of-the-Forest!" she said, draping it over the woman's shoulders.

Beloved-of-the-Forest's eyes widened. She hugged the cloth to her, unfolding the five yards in astonishment. Then she abruptly dropped the fabric on the ground, ran to the canoe, and returned with half a dozen small baskets. "More gift! You take!"

Elizabeth put out her hands. "I have no way to carry all the baskets. Jacob and I must walk home. You keep."

Beloved-of-the-Forest spoke to Walks Tall, then to Elizabeth. "Ride in canoe. Medicine Lady and Jacob."

"But it could be a long wait for Jacob," Elizabeth explained.

"We wait," Beloved-of-the-Forest assured her.

"Thank you. I'll be back," Elizabeth said. She returned to the main thoroughfare to look for Jacob, and finding no sign of him, wandered its length to the mill at the far end. Water from the river had been diverted for power. She listened to its plashing as it turned the wheel and ran on downstream, and wondered how much longer Jacob would need to work out a deal with Captain Winthrop.

Heading back to the general store, she settled onto the pine bench out front to wait some more. After what seemed like an hour—but was probably only half that long—Jacob returned. She knew from his staid expression that the meeting hadn't gone well. "When will Captain Winthrop take us to Detroit?" she asked anxiously.

Sitting beside her, he took her hand in his. "He'll be leaving Upper Saginaw in another day or two." He paused. After a long silence, he continued. "You'll have to go back to New York without me."

"What?" She pulled her hand free. "I don't understand! Won't Captain Winthrop take supplies in trade for our passage?"

"Yes—and no," Jacob replied.

"What kind of answer is that? Jacob, tell me what Captain Winthrop said!" Standing up, she started pacing back and forth.

From the corner of Jacob's eye, he caught a movement through the front window of the store, and realized the woman inside was eavesdropping. Taking Elizabeth by the elbow, he escorted her off the front step. "Captain Winthrop said passage home for the two of us was worth twice what we paid for our land. He'll take our supplies in trade for one fare, but he wants cash money for the other." Pausing, he faced Elizabeth, his hands on her shoulders. "Darling, I can't afford to go back to Brockport until I've made improvements to our land, and sold it."

Fuming, Elizabeth tried to argue. "But . . . but . . . "

Putting his finger to her lips, Jacob calmly said, "I tried every conceivable way to barter the price down. I even offered to deed over our land after I've cleared it and built a big, roomy log cabin on it. Captain Winthrop absolutely refused."

"I can't go home without you," Elizabeth reasoned, "and I hate Riverton too much to stay."

Jacob pulled her close, pressing his cheek into her silky hair. "That *is* a dilemma. But it's your choice to make. I guess you're the only one who can determine which is more important—being with me, or being free of Riverton." He kissed her forehead, then gazed into her sad brown eyes. "There's one thing I want you to know. If you go, I'll miss you more than the sun in the sky!"

The corners of her mouth tilted upward. "And I'll miss you more than the sun *and* the sky." She sighed. "Oh, Jacob, why does this have to be so difficult? How can you possibly expect me to decide? And so quickly. I suppose we have to let Captain Winthrop know before we leave Upper Saginaw."

Jacob put his arm about her waist. "He said to put up a

flag at Uncle Will's dock if we want him to stop. That gives you at least a day to figure out what you want to do. Now, we'd best head back. You'll probably want to rest a spell before you cook supper. Besides, that broken door of ours won't fix itself. Maybe I can get a start on it yet today." He stepped off in the direction of Riverton.

"Wait!" Elizabeth stopped abruptly. "I almost forgot. We don't have to walk home. Beloved-of-the-Forest and her husband, Walks Tall, offered to give us a ride back to Riverton in their canoe. They're waiting for us. Come on." Taking Jacob by the hand, she led him toward the river.

CHAPTER

4

On the way home, Elizabeth's frustration over the choice she faced seemed to increase with every stroke of Walks Tall's paddle. She was glad when Jacob asked the Indian to let them out before the Riverton dock, at the place where their lot met the rivershore. Beloved-of-the-Forest promised to deliver Elizabeth's baskets to their cabin, then the Chippewas pushed off and continued downriver.

Thankful for an opportunity to voice her thoughts privately to Jacob, Elizabeth made no secret whom she believed was to blame for the predicament of returning to New York alone. "It's all Uncle Will's fault, getting us stranded hundreds of miles from home. How could he possibly have thought we'd like it in Michigan?"

When Jacob made no reply, she continued. "He's just about the most deceitful, selfish man I've ever known—I'll take that back. He *is* the most deceitful and selfish man I've ever known. He'll do anything to sell people on Riverton, just to line his own pockets. Someday, he'll have to answer for all the grand stories he's told."

Jacob kept his counsel. Though he didn't believe his uncle was basically dishonest, he did think Will had gotten carried away with his enthusiasm for Riverton to the point of unwarranted exaggeration when promoting it to investors.

51

Pangs of hunger turned his thoughts from Will. His stomach grumbled so fiercely, he laughed out loud.

"How can you laugh at this dismal investment of ours?" Elizabeth challenged. "I'm so disgusted, I could just about tear down a tree with my bare hands."

Jacob refrained from comment until they had reached the opposite end of their property. "Look!" He pointed to three newly felled trees. "Uncle Will must have worked all day here."

Glancing about, Elizabeth replied, "And he's hardly put a dent in this forest."

"Never you mind," Jacob said, leading her along the trail to the cabin. "The job will get done, eventually."

"I don't know how you can be so optimistic," she muttered.

A few minutes later, Elizabeth stopped by Mrs. Clarke's to return her grass ropes. Jacob went ahead to get a start on repairing the broken door, but he stopped short the moment he came in sight of the cabin. The baskets Elizabeth had been promised stood outside, but to his surprise, the exterior appearance of the log home had changed considerably from when he and Elizabeth had left Riverton. Taking a look inside, he found even more astonishing changes. Instantly, he returned to the Clarkes'.

"Elizabeth, come quick!" He helped her up from the stump where she was seated and pulled her toward their cabin.

"Slow down, Jacob. My legs are so tired from walking to Upper Saginaw, then sitting on them all the way home in the canoe, I can hardly walk, let alone run to keep up with you."

With his arm tightly about her waist, he half carried her

along the trail.

Elizabeth drew a sharp breath the moment she saw the cabin door. The sheet Jacob had tacked up the night before had been taken down. In its place hung a solid plank door with a carved sign.

Jacob Morgan
Elizabeth Morgan, Medicine Lady

She approached the door, running her fingers in the grooves of the letters. "Jacob, who . . . ?"

"Look inside," he urged.

She pulled the latch string, pushed the door open a few inches and peeked in. Certain she was dreaming, she blinked several times, then swung the door wide open and stepped across the threshold. "We must be in the wrong place," she said, slowly taking in the improvements that seemed too good to be true.

"Not according to the sign on our door," Jacob reminded her.

"But who would have done this? And why?"

Sensing someone approaching, she turned to find Uncle Will standing behind her. Others in the community had come calling, too—the Langtons, Clarkes, Farrells, and Sayerses with their young ones, and even Mrs. Tyler and her little boy, who was clutching a handful of wildflowers.

Clara Langton stepped forth. "We heard you folks were planning to leave Riverton."

"I hope it's not too late to change your minds," said Mrs. Sayers.

Mrs. Clarke came inside and squeezed Elizabeth's hand. "I've been praying that you'll do what the Lord wants you to, even if it should mean living in a place you don't much like."

Mrs. Farrell entered next. "When your uncle told us this morning that you might not stay on, we all got busy. He made you this strong, new door. Even Brother-of-the-Wolf won't be able to break it." Resting her hand on a rocking chair that hadn't been there before, she said, "My husband finished this for you."

Mrs. Farrell's ten-year-old daughter, Naomi, joined her mother. "Papa was makin' it for Mama, but when he heard you might leave, he decided to give it to you and make Mama another one." Running her hand over the calico cushion that padded the rocker's seat, she added proudly, "And I sewed this cushion!"

"Try it out," Jacob said with a nudge.

The chair and cushion looked almost like what Elizabeth had seen in Upper Saginaw. When she sat down and rocked, the chair was every bit as comfortable. "Thank you Mr. Farrell, Naomi. This is the best chair I've ever owned."

Mrs. Sayers came forward to stand on a braided oval rug in the center of the room—beneath the repaired table and three rough-hewn, but serviceable chairs. "Louisa Tyler made this rag rug."

Elizabeth left the rocker to take a closer look. "It's lovely, Louisa, with its reds, blues, and greens—every color of the rainbow and more--but why not keep it for yourself?"

"I ain't got much use for it on my dirt floor. 'Sides, it's the least I can do in return for the vacc'nation ya gave me and my boy." To her son, she said, "Jeremy, give Mrs. Morgan the flowers ya picked for her." He buried his face in his mama's apron, then shyly came out from hiding to offer Elizabeth the bouquet.

She stooped down, accepting the wild roses, buttercups, and wild orchids. "Thank you, Jeremy. Thank you very much!"

Jacob took a mug from a new set of stoneware that had appeared on a new shelf, quickly ladled water into it for Elizabeth's flowers, and set them on the table.

Mrs. Sayers crossed the room, running her hand over a new quilt that had been spread on the bed. "Mrs. Langton and her girls, Jane and Ruth, pieced this sunshine and shadow quilt top. It kind of reflects the weather here in the Saginaw Valley. You never know one minute to the next what the day might bring."

"And Mrs. Sayers and her girl, Phoebe, quilted it all together," said Clara Langton. "They hung these new curtains for you, too." She indicated the red gingham tied back at the windows on either side of the cabin.

Elizabeth took a close look at the fine stitchery on the quilt, her heart full of gratitude. When she gazed up at the curtains, her eyes were too misty to focus. She brushed away the moisture and tried to speak past the lump in her throat. "Everything is . . . lovely. Thank you."

Jacob put his arm about her. Resting his hand on the back of one of the new chairs, he said, "I'd like to know who made these, who repaired the table, and who gave us a new shelf and brand new dishes?"

Captain Langton spoke up. "Those are compliments of your Uncle Will, too, same as the provisions setting over there in the corner—a sack of flour, another of cornmeal, and a firkin of salt pork."

Despite Elizabeth's belief that Uncle Will owed them

these supplies, and more, if he were ever to make amends for his deceptions about Riverton, she cleared her throat and offered a polite, "Thank you, Uncle Will."

"You're welcome, niece."

She nearly choked at his claim to the relationship, if only by marriage, and was thankful when Mrs. Clarke came forward, placing a doily on the table beneath the stoneware mug full of flowers.

"I didn't have much chance to contribute, what with Brother-of-the-Wolf in such a bad state, but I'd like for you to have this. I made it years ago, and it does pretty things up a bit."

"I'll cherish it, you can be sure," Elizabeth said.

"And I almost forgot," Mrs. Clarke continued. Pulling a small tin from her pocket and setting it on the table, she explained, "Here's a little tea for you and Jacob. My special mix of China's best."

"We'll savor every cupful," Elizabeth assured her.

A moment followed when no one seemed to know what to say next, then Will's loud, gravelly voice broke the silence. "Well, it's near time to eat. Haven't you ladies got pots to tend to? And you men—help me set up a plank table on some sawhorses down at the blockhouse so we can get this community supper underway." To Jacob and Elizabeth, he said, "You two are the guests of honor, being our newest residents. Just come on down with a place setting each of those new dishes I gave you, and don't bother bringing anything to pass."

When supper had ended and Jacob had wandered off to talk with Uncle Will and Captain Langton, Elizabeth started gathering together their dirty dishes. She had nearly finished setting them in a neat stack when Mrs. Farrell, Mrs. Langton, Mrs. Sayers, and their daughters approached her.

"Mrs. Morgan, might we have a word with you? It'll only take a minute," Mrs. Langton said. "Your uncle claims you got a good bit of book learning back in York State, what with your father being a doctor and all, and we were wondering. Seeing as how you're a good deal more educated than any of us, do you think you could spend a few hours a week teaching our girls—if you stay on?"

"Just informal-like," said Mrs. Farrell. "Naomi longs to go to school, but it'll likely be a good long while 'fore Riverton gets a schoolhouse of its own. Upper Saginaw don't even have one yet, and there's a good deal more younguns there than here."

"My Phoebe knows how to read—a little," Mrs. Sayers said proudly. "She'd be most appreciative of any time ya spent with her. Mightn't be ya could even teach her to write—if ya stay a piece in Riverton."

"I'd be a good student, I promise!" Phoebe insisted.

The eager look in her eyes, the hopeful expressions of Mrs. Sayers and the other mothers and daughters, touched Elizabeth deeply. Working with the girls would help to return the many kindnesses they had already shown her and Jacob, if she should decide to stay.

"I haven't ever taught anyone," Elizabeth explained, "but I'd be glad to give it a try—if I stay."

"Thank you, Mrs. Morgan!" said Phoebe, hugging Elizabeth tightly, as if she'd already agreed to remain in Riverton permanently.

"Yes, thank you!" said Mrs. Sayers.

"You let me know what hours you want to see the girls just as soon as you've decided," said Clara Langton.

"You're a real blessing to Riverton!" Mrs. Farrell told her.

As the women and their daughters moved off, Jacob joined Elizabeth again. "What was that all about?"

"The women wanted to know if I'd teach their daughters." She pulled her shawl over her shoulders while Jacob picked up the stack of dishes.

"And what did you say?"

"I said I didn't have any experience, but if I stay in Riverton, I'll give it a try."

"You'd make a fine teacher." Shifting the dishes to one side, Jacob put his arm about her waist. "Now let's go home and get some rest. This has been a long day."

"Yes, it has," said Elizabeth, pausing to yawn. "But it had a very nice ending. I'm eager to get back to the cabin and admire our new gifts one more time before I turn in."

When Elizabeth arrived home, she sat down in her rocker and simply gazed about the room, sensing the coziness that had set in with the addition of the curtains and rug, chairs and shelves, quilt and flowers. She said a small prayer of thanks for her neighbors' generosity, knowing how dearly it had cost them in this remote wilderness.

She pondered the question of teaching the girls in Riverton, then she got up from the rocker and started to undress for bed.

Jacob came beside her, wrapping his arms loosely about her waist and turning her toward him. Having seen the meditative look on her face for the past half hour, he was certain she had been wrestling with the question of returning to Brockport.

"I love you, my darling," he said tenderly. Then he dropped a kiss on her nose, and one on her lips that deepened until he ended it a minute later. Savoring every precious second of her nearness, he reluctantly asked, "Have you decided about tomorrow . . . about the *Governor Marcy?*"

She simply gazed at him, her expression one of uncertainty—or was it regret? Then a peaceful look came over her, and she almost smiled. "I've been praying for guidance, and God has answered my prayer. I'm going to stay on until Fall. You'll probably sell our land by then, and we'll be able to return to Brockport together. In any case, I'm leaving Michigan before winter sets in. I can't imagine surviving the cold and snow in this cabin."

A weight lifted from Jacob's heart, and he picked her up and turned about, almost giddy with happiness. "I'll do my best to make your stay comfortable, my darling. How I love you!" Pressing his lips firmly to hers, he indulged in an embrace that lasted long after he had laid her down on the pine needle mattress.

Several days later, Jacob stood back, wiped the sweat from his brow, and looked with pride at the clearing he and his uncle had made. The cabin site was banked by the river, and surrounded by stately pines atwitter with the songs of finches and sparrows. Popping a piece of peppermint stick into his mouth, he leaned against his axe and gazed at the pile of logs at the rear of the lot. Out of that timber, he and Will would build a cabin, and once constructed, this Riverton parcel would be very appealing to newcomers, Jacob was certain. By October, he and Elizabeth would be on their way East.

The thought made him sad. He'd really come to enjoy the Saginaw Valley, and his work clearing trees. He looked forward to putting up the cabin—his first experience with construction. Such feelings made him realize he had adjusted quickly to the challenges of wilderness life, and had no real desire to return to the formal suits and stuffy banker's office of Brockport.

His uncle, who had been down to the river to refresh himself after a hard day's toil, ambled back to the lot, resting his boot on a nearby stump. "Tomorrow we can start digging the foundation for your new house, Jacob."

He swallowed the last of his candy and corrected his uncle. "You mean the cabin."

Will's head moved from side to side. "Now that you've gone to the trouble of clearing such a pretty site, you ought to build something substantial on it. You'll get a lot more for your land when you sell it, if you've put up a frame house, rather than one of those twelve-by-twenty-four-foot cabins."

"But that will take lumber, and you know I can't afford to go to the mill with my logs."

Will shrugged off the argument. "I can get credit at the mill in Upper Saginaw. When you've finished the house and sold it, you can pay me what you owe, and I'll take care of the debt at the mill. You'll have plenty more money to take with you to Brockport--if you ever go back there--than if you build a cabin. The way prices are going, a new house in these parts is one of the best investments a man can make!"

Jacob grinned. "You're a real joker, Uncle Will. Elizabeth would be beside herself with anger if she thought I'd gone into debt with you to build a house. She still thinks it's *you* who owes *us!* And she's made it very clear she won't stay in Riverton through the winter."

Will smiled mischievously. "She needn't know about your debt, or the house—not right away, anyhow. If we're careful, she won't find out till it's too late. Once the house is finished, she just might like it well enough to change her mind and stay. It was the cabin she objected to for wintering over."

Jacob pondered his uncle's tempting proposal, trying to sort out the possibilities. "If I *did* start building a house, there's no way I could keep it a secret from Elizabeth. She's bound to come by here one of these days, even if she *has* been staying clear of us since her trip to Upper Saginaw. But you never know when trouble might come along—like smallpox—and send her straight to us."

"She needn't come here to get our help. Just tell her to ring the bell at the blockhouse, and we'll come running. It's dangerous work, building a cabin—too dangerous for women to come near."

Jacob was still thinking through his uncle's logic when Will spoke again. "Tell you what, Jacob. Tomorrow, we can start on the foundation. That much won't cost you anything but a lame back. Once that's done, you can decide if you want to go ahead with the house, or simply put a cabin on it."

Jacob nodded. "No need to rush into a decision. I'll see you tomorrow morning."

As he headed down to the river to wash up, a sense of excitement grew within at the prospect of building a frame house—the first in Riverton. But as he walked the trail toward home, he couldn't shake the guilty feeling, knowing that Elizabeth would never agree to such a proposal and if he pursued it, he would have to do so without her knowledge. Still, it wouldn't hurt to emphasize the importance of her staying away from the lot, and the availability of the bell at the blockhouse for summoning him.

On a warm afternoon near the end of July, when Elizabeth was certain she had correctly diagnosed the reason for the interruption in her monthly feminine pattern, she decided to pay Mrs. Clarke a call. Despite her experience, helping her father to treat women who were in the family way, she longed for a woman-to-woman discussion about her condition, and she dared not speak of it with the mothers of her students. Certainly, word would spread quickly of the impending birth, and she wasn't ready for that. She trusted Mrs. Clarke not to betray her secret.

As she followed the trail to her neighbor's, the essence of green wood smoke stung her nose. It was a common sight, rising from the direction of the lot she and Jacob owned. Evidently, he and Will were still burning the refuse from the trees they had felled. Nearby, chipmunks scolded her, then darted after one another, crossing the path only two feet in front of her. She smiled at their antics, and the thought struck her that she would miss such wilderness entertainments when she returned to Brockport.

However, return she would, especially with the new development taking place in her life. As she pulled the latch string on Mrs. Clarke's door, she was thankful to have such a good neighbor and friend to whom she could turn for advice. She had started to open the door when she heard someone urgently call her name.

She turned to find Louisa running toward her. As the woman paused to catch her breath, Elizabeth couldn't help noticing her hair was more disheveled than normal, and her eyes—full of fright—bore dark circles beneath.

"Mrs. Tyler, what's the matter?"

"It's Zeb . . . " She paused to catch her breath.

Mrs. Clarke opened her door wide. "Louisa, is Zeb in his cups again?" she asked, putting her arm about the woman's shoulders.

Louisa shook her head vigorously. Tears welling in her eyes, she blurted out, "He's sick. *Real* sick. Fact is, I think he's . . . dead!"

CHAPTER

5

Louisa began to cry.

"I'll get my bag," Elizabeth said. "You take Mrs. Clarke, and go on home."

A few minutes later, Elizabeth entered the Tyler's mean, dingy cabin. A gray, wolf-like puppy with black feet greeted her. It took a moment for her eyes to adjust to the dim light, then she saw Zeb Tyler sprawled out on a bed, Louisa and Mrs. Clarke by his side.

Elizabeth bent over her patient. Pock marks were obvious on his face as she felt for breath from his nostrils. Certain he had stopped breathing, she unbuttoned his work shirt and knelt down to listen to his heart, his foul-smelling undershirt making her stomach turn.

"Can ya help him?" Louisa asked anxiously.

Elizabeth rose and shook her head. "I'm sorry, Mrs. Tyler. Your husband has died of smallpox."

Louisa sobbed openly. "I knew he shoulda taken the vaccine."

"There, now," Mrs. Clarke soothed. "'Twas nothing you could do to change that."

Elizabeth draped a soiled sheet over the body as she spoke to the widow. "I'll call the others together. Mrs. Clarke will stay with you for now."

Making haste to the blockhouse, Elizabeth rang the bell

64

furiously. Jacob and Will were the first to arrive.

"What is it, Elizabeth?" Jacob asked. "Is someone hurt?"

"Was there an accident?" Will wanted to know.

"No, no accident. Mr. Tyler has just died of smallpox."

Jacob slowly shook his head. "If anyone should have had that vaccination, he should have."

Will removed his cap and slapped it against his thigh in frustration. "I knew it! Something like that was bound to happen. Jacob, we'd better organize the men, some to make the coffin, others to dig the grave."

As folks began to gather, Elizabeth told Will and Jacob, "I'll let Louisa know you're making burial preparations, and ask Mrs. Clarke to summon the Reverend from the Indian village."

She returned to the Tylers to stay with Louisa. After awhile, two men came for the corpse.

Mrs. Langton arrived soon after, letting herself in by the latchstring to speak with Louisa. "The men will bury your husband tomorrow afternoon, then the ladies will serve a dinner down at the blockhouse. For the next couple of days, we're going to take turns staying with you, till you're over the worst of it."

Tears spilled down Louisa's cheeks. "Thanks, Clara. I don't know what I'd do without ya—and Mrs. Morgan, of course."

"We'll take care of things," Mrs. Langton assured her.

Three days later, after her students had been dismissed, Elizabeth spent hours simmering chowder—the same recipe Mrs. Langton had used when she had brought supper to her on her first night in Riverton. Herbs gathered from the forest sent a pleasant aroma throughout the cabin, mingling nicely with the pike Elizabeth had purchased from the Indians. When it was done, she took a pot of the soup to the Tylers, encountering Will outside their cabin, splitting wood and arranging it in a neat pile. A wolf-like puppy raced toward her, jumping up against her apron.

"Down, Blackfoot!" Will commanded.

Immediately, the dog sat.

"Good boy. Stay." Will patted his head as he spoke to Elizabeth. "I sure feel bad for the Widow Tyler. Zeb didn't even leave enough firewood to last her a week, that lazy bum!" He picked up a chip of wood and sent it flying into the forest. The dog chased after it, then settled down to chew it apart.

Elizabeth focused on Will. "I'm sure Louisa appreciates your help. I've brought her some chowder."

"Let me take that for you." Will reached for the pot, lifting the lid slightly to inhale the aroma. "Mmm. You're getting to be a right smart cook, Elizabeth."

"There's plenty there for you, too," she said, pulling the latch string to open the door.

Will followed her inside where Louisa and Jeremy were playing with wooden blocks at the table. To Elizabeth's surprise, the tired, haggard look had nearly disappeared from the widow's face, and her hair had been brushed and fashioned into a neat twist at the nape of her neck. A modest black frock replaced her everyday patched calico dress.

"Elizabeth's brought supper," Will announced, setting the pot on the hearth.

Jeremy squealed happily, got down from his chair and ran to Will, hugging his legs. Will picked him up, gave him a hug in return, and set him back on his chair. "I've got to get back to work. Why don't you ladies chat a minute."

"Please make yourself to home," said Louisa, offering Elizabeth a chair.

"I can't stay long," said Elizabeth, stepping forward onto wood this time instead of dirt. Someone had begun to install puncheon flooring, and she noticed that at the back of the cabin, light filtered through a newly installed six-paned glass window. Before she could stop herself, she said, "My, things have certainly changed here in the last two days."

Louisa offered a self-conscious smile. "Your uncle put in the window and started to lay flooring for me today. He's just about the kindest man I ever did know." Her eyes began welling with tears. "You Morgans have been awful good to me. I know I can't make up for all you've done, but if ever there's any way I can return a favor, you'll let me know, won't ya?" She brushed away a tear with her apron.

A thought came to Elizabeth. "As a matter of fact, there *is* something you can do. I can see that pretty soon, you're going to need the rag rug you gave me. If I bring you enough scraps, could you make me another one to replace it?"

Louisa nodded eagerly. "Sure 'nough."

Elizabeth smiled. "Good. Now, I'd best be on my way. Jacob will be wanting supper. We'll visit again soon," she promised, letting herself out. Will was stacking wood alongside the cabin, and she waved to him as she started down the cross trail toward home, thinking as she went that there was more to his concern for Louisa than just a matter of sympathy over her loss.

*   *   *

As Elizabeth set the table for dinner and stirred the pot of beans she had been simmering all day, she pondered how to break the news to Jacob that a blessed event would be coming in the Morgan family. A week had passed since the day after the Tyler funeral, when she had been able to share her news with Mrs. Clarke, and finding the right time to tell Jacob had proved far more difficult.

It seemed he was either working at their Riverton lot with Uncle Will, or too tired to be attentive. Each of the past few evenings, he had eaten supper with great dispatch, then immediately dropped off to sleep. Mornings, he rose early, tip-toed out of the cabin, and headed down to the blockhouse where Will cooked him a hearty breakfast.

Though Elizabeth would have preferred rising early and cooking his breakfast herself, she had accepted the alternative arrangement because of the fatigue that had set in with her condition. As a result, she had been unable to find the tender moments required for revealing news of a pending birth.

She had sat down in her rocker to take up the booties she had started knitting that morning, and give further thought to the problem, when Louisa and Jeremy pulled the latchstring on her door and stepped inside, each of them bearing brown paper packages.

"We wouldna come so close to mealtime, 'cept I was mighty certain the Morgan men 'd be workin' late again tonight," Louisa explained. "'Sides, Jeremy and me just finished gettin' these things ready for ya this afternoon, and couldn't wait to bring 'em over."

Elizabeth rose to greet them. "How nice of you to come. Won't you sit a minute?" She indicated the chairs at the table.

"Just for a minute," said Louisa, setting her package on the table, then sitting down and lifting Jeremy onto her lap.

Elizabeth sat, too.

Giving Jeremy a nudge, Louisa said, "Go on now, son. Give Mrs. Morgan your present." Shyly, he set it on the table. "Good boy," Louisa said, shoving both parcels in Elizabeth's direction.

"This is quite a surprise," Elizabeth said. "You needn't have brought me anything, but I do love presents."

"Open! Open!" the boy demanded.

Elizabeth inspected his parcel. "I can't imagine what this is. It's too small to be the rag rug," she concluded as she slipped off the string. She unfolded the paper to find a white flannel baby kimono finely embroidered with tiny blue and pink flowers. A warmth invaded her face. "How did you know I'm . . . I've only told Mrs. Clarke."

Louisa grinned broadly. "Now don't go blamin' her for spillin' a secret. I noticed certain things about ya lately. Signs of change a-comin'." Pushing her own parcel closer, she said, "Now open this one."

Quickly, Elizabeth dispensed with the wrapping, discovering a dozen flannel diapers.

"I know ya won't have need of 'em for a long while. By the time ya do, you'll be back East. But after all the nice things ya done for me, I wanted to do somethin' special in return—somethin' besides that rug I'm makin' ya."

Elizabeth reached out, laying her hand atop Louisa's. "Thank you so very much. I surely appreciate your efforts."

Louisa smiled. "When y'r tendin' y'r little one, I want ya to think of me 'n Jeremy, and be as happy as I am with my little boy." She hugged her son and kissed him on the head.

"I will, Mrs. Tyler. That, I can assure you." As she admired the gifts again, her thoughts turned to Jacob. "You know, I haven't found the right time to tell my husband yet. I'd appreciate it if you wouldn't mention this to anyone for awhile." A troubling notion struck her. "Will doesn't know, does he?"

Louisa shook her head. "I did tell your uncle I had a need of five yards of white flannel. Next day, he showed up with it, but he didn't ask what it was for, and I didn't tell him." A moment lapsed, then Louisa laughed softly. "I remember, I didn't know how to tell Zeb when I was carryin' Jeremy. Finally, I just set out some diapers and a baby bonnet, and he got the hint all right." Setting Jeremy down, she said, "Well, we've gotta be on our way, now. The fellas 'll be showin' up any minute, wantin' their vittles."

Elizabeth saw her guests to the door. "Thanks again, for all you've done. We'll talk again soon."

"Now it's your turn to come callin' at my place, and don't ya dare bring a thing!" Louisa said.

"I'll come by," Elizabeth promised, closing the door behind her guests.

She laid the baby diapers and kimono over Jacob's chair, stirred the beans, and sat again in her rocker to take up her knitting. She had completed several more rows, and was wondering what had delayed Jacob's return, when the distant sound of thunder portended a storm. As time passed, and the thunder grew louder, she put away her handiwork, moved the beans off to the side to keep them warm, and took the lantern from the wall.

Outdoors, the sky had grown dark with encroaching rain clouds. The air was damp, and full of hungry mosquitoes. Elizabeth swatted constantly at them as she hurried along the path toward the land where Jacob was building a cabin. As she neared the blockhouse, she decided to check there for Jacob and Will. Approaching the heavy door, she lifted the latch and swung it wide open, holding her lantern high.

"Hello, anybody there?" she called. A muffled noise made her curious, and she stepped into the dim storage room to take a better look.

"Hello," she called again. A scratching noise came in response. Then a whoosh sounded from behind, and something brushed her shoulders. Heart racing, she turned to run out the door, catching sight of an owl landing on the loft with its prey, a mouse. "You sure startled me," she scolded, stepping outside and bolting the door. The rope to the bell was swinging in the wind, and she considered sounding an emergency alarm, but decided against it until she had gone at least as far as the lot, certain she would find Jacob there.

Huge pines towered over her, rustling in the breeze as she went. Gusts of wind sent shadows swaying to darken her path as thunder increased in the distance. Approaching the lot, she remembered how time and again, Jacob had warned her not to go there because of the danger, but she couldn't ignore the voice of intuition that pushed her on.

When she reached the clearing, a bolt of lightning revealed a startling image—the structure of a frame house!

A fierce gust of wind rattled the glass in her lantern. Holding tight with both hands, she proceeded toward the foundation.

"Jacob! Jacob, where are you?" she called frantically. Rain splattered against her face, then a brighter bolt of lightning lit the sky. In one terrifying moment, she saw a huge pine beginning to split apart—only a few feet from where Jacob was standing!

"Jacob, watch out!" Elizabeth shouted.

The tree creaked and groaned. In the darkness, it crashed to the ground.

"Jacob! Are you all right?" she cried. "Answer me!" She continued in the direction of the split tree. Rain poured down, soaking her shoes with mud and splashing it against the hem of her skirt. She had almost reached the damaged tree when she nearly stumbled over his inert form.

Kneeling down, she cradled his head in her arms. "Jacob! Wake up!" she demanded. She checked his nostril, and felt the warmth of his breathing. "Thank God, you're alive!" she cried. "Wake up! You've got to wake up!" she insisted, shaking his shoulders. When he didn't respond, she began to sob, and pray. "Dear Lord, how am I ever going to get Jacob home?"

She sensed someone behind her and turned to find Brother-of-the-Wolf kneeling down.

"Me help Medicine Lady!" Carefully, he lifted Jacob's limp form, draped him over one shoulder, and strode swiftly toward the trail that would take them to the LaMore cabin.

Elizabeth trotted behind, rain soaking her hair and streaming down her face. As she went, she prayed for Jacob's recovery. A few minutes later, she pushed open the cabin door for Brother-of-the-Wolf.

He laid Jacob on the bed and Elizabeth immediately tried to rouse him with smelling salts. Getting no response, she set to work removing his soaked shirt and pants. Checking for injuries, she found one knee beginning to swell, but no serious damage. Putting his dry nightshirt on him, she covered him with the quilt.

Barely conscious of her own damp clothing, she pulled a crude chair alongside the bed and sat down, taking Jacob's hand in hers. Bowing her head, she prayed silently for God's healing powers, and His guidance in caring for her injured husband. When she opened her eyes, Brother-of- the-Wolf was crouched beside her, holding her Bible out to her.

"Thank you," she said, taking the book from him, "and thank you for bringing Jacob home."

He nodded, then sat on the floor beside her, legs crossed. His continued presence making her uncomfortable, she asked, "Would you like something to eat? Beans?" Gesturing toward the pot by the fire, she said, "Help yourself. Eat all you want."

He ignored her offer, focusing instead on the unopened Bible in her hand. An awkward moment lapsed, then he spoke. "Pastor Ben teach Brother-of-the-Wolf from Good Book. Now, Brother-of-the-Wolf no drink alcohol. Brother-of-the-Wolf sorry for what he did when drunk. Medicine Lady saved Chippewa from sickness. Brother-of-the-Wolf thank Medicine Lady. Brother-of-the-Wolf ask forgiveness for his bad deeds."

Elizabeth searched Brother-of-the-Wolf's dark eyes, finding a look of true repentance. "I forgive you, Brother-of-the-Wolf. Have you asked forgiveness from God?"

Without hesitation, he nodded. "In times past, Brother-of-the-Wolf ask forgiveness of Gitchie Manitou, Great Spirit of Chippewas. Now, Brother-of-the-Wolf asks

Father God. In times past, Brother-of-the-Wolf walked with Gitchie Manitou. Now, Brother-of-the-Wolf walks with Father God."

Elizabeth smiled. "You've come a long way in learning about God, Brother-of-the-Wolf. I'll pray for you, that you always walk with your Father in heaven."

The staid line of his mouth curved upward ever-so-slightly, then he rose and let himself out into the stormy night.

Elizabeth said a silent prayer of thanks for the changes in Brother-of-the-Wolf. Tucking the sunshine and shadow quilt more snugly about Jacob, she realized how accurately the pattern reflected this day of extremes. As she changed from her damp clothing to her dry nightgown and wrapper, she saw in her mind the pitched roof of a frame house revealed by the bolt of lightning, and wondered how Jacob could have started construction on such a project with their limited resources, and without even telling her!

She suspected Uncle Will had something to do with it, but she knew the answer would have to wait. Putting away the chair, she pulled her comfortable rocker beside the bed and rocked herself to sleep. Hours of fitful slumber passed before she fell into a deeper, more refreshing sleep. When she awoke, bright sunlight was streaming in the east window, and Jacob was propped up on his elbow, staring at her.

"Jacob! You're awake!" she cried joyfully.

He started to get up, his face contorting with pain.

She pressed him down with a firm hand. "Stay put, Jacob. Medicine Lady's orders. I've been worried sick about you."

The painful expression disappeared, and one corner of

74

his mouth turned upward. "I can see that. I'm sorry. I don't know what happened. I remember working late with Uncle Will. Then the storm started to come up and he left. I stayed behind to take care of . . . everything is black after that."

"Oh, Jacob!" Elizabeth sat on the bed beside him and threw her arms about his neck.

He held her tight, kissing her hair, her cheek her mouth. When the kiss ended, he fixed his gaze on her. "Something's on your mind, I can tell."

Several moments lapsed before she responded. "Jacob, last night when the storm came up and you hadn't come home, I went looking for you at our lot. Why didn't you tell me you're building a frame house?"

He reached for her hand. "I was going to tell you. Honest. I just hadn't found the right time."

She wrenched free and pushed off the bed. Taking the diapers and kimono from the back of his chair, she held them out for him to see. "And I hadn't found the right time to tell you about this. I'm going to have a baby, Jacob. And I'm not going to have it in the wilderness!" Overcome with emotion, she turned away, burying her face in the soft flannel to hide her tears.

"A baby," Jacob repeated in wonder. Getting up off the bed, he nearly fell when his right leg buckled beneath his weight. He leaned against a chair and put his arm about Elizabeth, her back to him as she sobbed softly.

Jacob's touch made Elizabeth cry all the more, realizing she was caught in a web of love for him, and the knowledge of his betrayal. When her tears had subsided, she laid the baby clothes on the table and stepped out of his embrace, turning to face him. "Jacob . . . " she struggled to speak past the lump in her throat. "Sometimes I wish I didn't love you so much. Then it wouldn't hurt so when . . . the disappointments come." Gaining better control, she added, "I know why you're building a house instead of a cabin. You think it will change my mind about Riverton, that I'll want to stay."

He started to reach for her, falling when his knee gave out. She caught him, easing him onto a chair. He pulled up the hem of his nightshirt to reveal a kneecap twice its normal size.

She inspected the swelling, then focused on the man who had brought her both sunshine and shadows in the space of a few minutes. "Your knee will heal in time Jacob. But I can't promise you there will ever come a time when I'll want to stay permanently in Riverton. I can't tolerate Uncle Will interfering in our affairs. The house was his idea, wasn't it?"

A long moment later, Jacob replied, "He bartered at the mill in Upper Saginaw for the lumber. When it's finished, we'll be able to sell it for several times my investment, provided you don't want to stay. The house was a sound idea, Elizabeth."

"And your not telling me—was that a sound idea, too?"

Jacob hung his head.

Elizabeth rose. "Jacob," she tipped his chin until his gaze met hers, "I hope one day you'll realize that our honesty with one another will pay far more dividends than secret investments in things of this world."

CHAPTER

6

Rain fell steadily throughout the day, confining Elizabeth to the cabin. With classes canceled, the hours passed on lead feet. While Jacob rested and read a bound copy of *The Cabinet of Natural History and American Rural Sports*, she continued knitting the pair of baby booties she had begun the day before. The midday meal was small, with Jacob's appetite fit only for a cup of broth. Elizabeth was thankful when the supper hour drew near, and his appetite had improved sufficiently for her to prepare a full meal. She was frying salt pork to go with her beans and corncakes when Uncle Will let himself in, a leather portfolio beneath his arm. She set the frying pan away from the flame and covered it to keep it warm, then turned to speak to the man she wanted least to see in her home.

Will spoke first. "Brother-of-the-Wolf told me about the accident last night. I'm sorry you got hurt, Jacob."

"My knee's pretty bad," he explained, hobbling to one of the chairs at the table. "I won't be able to work for a few days."

"Well, I've brought something to make you feel better!" Will hung up his wet hat and cape, took off his boots, and crossed the puncheon floor in stockinged feet. Setting his portfolio on the table, he turned his attention to Elizabeth. "Sit down with us, niece. I want to tell you about a decision I've come to."

Reluctantly, she complied.

From his portfolio, Will extracted several legal documents, and a map of Riverton. Focusing on Elizabeth, he said, "I took to heart your point about the price you paid for your parcel of land. Maybe I did exaggerate just a tad about the developments of the community. I'd hate for you to go back to Brockport feeling cheated." Pointing to the map of Riverton, he indicated five x's either side of the lot where Jacob was building the house. "I'm deeding over these ten parcels to do with what you wish." With a flourish, he shoved the deeds across the table.

Elizabeth studied them. They looked authentic, like the one Jacob already held for the lot he had bought months ago. "But . . . what about the supplies?" Elizabeth asked. "You promised we could have supplies equal to the payment on our land as barter for passage East?"

"If you decide to return East, they're yours to barter. Of course, now that you and Jacob are big land holders here in Riverton, I'm hoping you'll change your mind about leaving."

"So you're bribing me to stay," Elizabeth concluded.

"No, indeed!" Will insisted. "I'm giving you the land because it's the right thing to do."

Jacob smiled broadly. "Thanks very much, Uncle Will!" Taking the documents from Elizabeth, he jogged them together. "Now, my darling, my appetite has improved immensely in the past few minutes. Would you be kind enough to set three places and serve up supper?"

"Of course," she said. "You'll stay, won't you, Uncle Will?" she asked, secretly hoping he'd decline in case Louisa was expecting him for the evening meal.

"I'd be honored!" he replied, closing his portfolio and setting it beneath his chair.

While Elizabeth tended to the pork, beans, and corn-cakes, she listened to the conversation between Will and Jacob flowing with possibilities for the land Jacob had just acquired—clearing it for a vegetable garden; selling it to pay for services at the saw mill; putting up a cabin on speculation. Despite the sincerity that seemed to surround Will's magnanimous gesture, Elizabeth couldn't help wondering if something more lay behind his newly acquired generosity.

When the meal had ended and Will was donning his cape and boots, he paused to face Elizabeth. "Before I leave, there's something I need to ask you and Jacob," he said. "Louisa—the Widow Tyler—and I would like the pleasure of your company for dinner at the Western Hotel in Upper Saginaw a week from next Saturday. We can set out by canoe at about two in the afternoon, if that suits."

Jacob spoke from the back of the cabin, where he was resting on the bed. "Elizabeth, are you willing? It would be a pleasant trip in good weather, and easy on the shoe leather."

"I'll tell you straight out, Elizabeth," Will said, "several men in the area have planned a meeting there to talk about ways of bringing more settlers into the Saginaw Valley. You should bring your handiwork and plan to stay over until Sunday. It's likely our discussion will last well into the night."

"It would be a nice change for you, darling," Jacob said.

When Elizabeth made no reply, Will spoke again. "Louisa would be mighty disappointed not to have your company."

Following a moment's further consideration, Elizabeth said, "Tell Louisa I'm looking forward to the trip."

"She'll be glad to hear it! Good night!"

As Will stepped out into the damp evening air, Elizabeth noticed that the rain had let up and a rainbow was starting to form. Perhaps it was a sign that her future in Riverton was truly changing for the better.

"Are you really gonna move East again, Mrs. Morgan?" ten-year-old Naomi Farrell asked one morning a few days later, after Elizabeth had taught a class on geography. She was sitting at her table with Naomi and her other students. In the center was the map Elizabeth had drawn on Jane Langton's slate board showing New York, the Erie Canal, the lakes, and Michigan. Each girl had marked the town from which she had come, and now understood the route bringing settlers by the thousands into the Midwest.

"Yeah, are ya really gonna go away for good?" nine-year-old Phoebe Sayers wanted to know, "'cause if ya do, I'm gonna feel so bad, even my hair is gonna hurt."

"Hair doesn't have feelings," said twelve-year-old Ruth Langton, tugging on Phoebe's braid.

"Ouch! It does too!"

"That was your *scalp* that hurt, not your hair," said Ruth's thirteen-year-old sister, Jane. "Hair is dead. That's why you can cut it and you don't feel anything. Isn't that right, Mrs. Morgan?"

"I'd never really thought of it that way, Jane, but what you said makes sense," Elizabeth replied. Her oldest students, Jane and Ruth Langton, were a constant challenge, and she'd learned to prepare well for the twice-weekly two-hour classes in order to keep ahead of them.

Naomi spoke again. "Maybe Jane makes sense, Mrs. Morgan, but I don't make no sense—"

"*Any* sense, Naomi."

"*Any* sense of your goin' back East when so many folks is comin' West. Besides, I want ya to be my teacher all year long. And next year, too."

"And the year after that!" Phoebe Sayers added.

Elizabeth checked the time on the watch Jacob left with her twice a week on class days so she could start and end her sessions promptly. "I see it's time for closing prayer. We'll talk about it again next time. Jane, would you like to lead the prayer?"

Jane bowed her head and the other girls did likewise, clasping hands. Naomi and Phoebe, on either side of Elizabeth, squeezed her hands more tightly than on other days.

"Dear heavenly Father," Jane began reverently, "thank you for our time together to learn. Be with each of us until we meet again. And God, if it's not asking too much, could you convince Mrs. Morgan to stay on here so we can keep learning? In Jesus' name, Amen."

"Amen," said the other girls.

"We'll meet again next week, Tuesday," Elizabeth said, rising to see the girls out. After a cloudy start, the day had turned sunny, and a breeze brought the fresh scent of pine through the open door. In the distance, she could hear hammers pounding, making her eager to visit Jacob and Will to see their progress on the house—a routine she had been following each of the past few days since Jacob had recovered from his accident and returned to work. Perhaps she would even take along some cornbread and smoked fish and make a picnic of the midday meal.

Her thoughts were interrupted when Jane Langton paused on her way out, her slate held carefully so as not to spoil the map Elizabeth had drawn. "Mrs. Morgan, do you have any books about doctoring? I want to learn all about doctoring like you did."

Elizabeth shook her head. "I'm sorry, Jane. The books I learned from all belong to my father, and he keeps them on a shelf in his office in Brockport so he can look things up when he's having trouble figuring out what's wrong with his patients."

"Oh." Jane looked down at her slate.

An idea came to Elizabeth. "Jane, why don't you do what I did when I first started learning about doctoring. If your papa brings home a fish, tell him you'll clean it, then cut it open carefully and study what's inside. If your papa kills a deer, watch him when he cuts open the gut. Then draw what you see on your slate and come show me. We'll talk about it."

Jane's face brightened. "I used to study the innards of the chickens and pigs Mama killed for us to eat back East. She told me what the different parts were, as much as she knew, but I bet you know a whole lot more. Thanks, Mrs. Morgan! I'm going to pay real close attention the next time Papa goes hunting!" She skipped down the trail toward home.

Quickly, Elizabeth gathered together some pieces of leftover cornbread, berries not eaten at breakfast, and the smoked whitefish Beloved-of-the-Forest had recently given her. She set the food in an Indian basket along with tin cups, gingham napkins, and a jar of water, and headed for the sound of the hammers. Even before she reached the building site, she could see through the treetops that great progress had been made on the roof, its shingles nearly all in place on one side. Entering the clearing, the pleasing scent of raw wood drifted her way.

"Jacob!" she called above the din of the hammers.

He waved to her, then climbed down, along with Will.

Kissing her on the cheek, he said proudly, "We ought to finish shingling the roof today."

"Then we can start on the siding," said Will. "Once that's on, this place will look so much like a house, you'll want to move right in, Elizabeth!"

Jacob spoke again. "You want white siding with green shutters, don't you, darling?"

Elizabeth chuckled. "Yes, for what it's worth. But you're a long way from painting." Even so, she could easily envision the white clapboard, the six-pane windows where their frames had been set in place, and the solid door that would be hung at the front. Despite its state of unreadiness, the shape of the house reminded her of her father's. She stepped up onto the front stoop and went inside.

Jacob joined her, taking her by the hand and drawing her farther into the entryway. "I thought I'd finish the foyer just like your father's, with plaster painted pale green, and dark walnut up to about here." He indicated a place about three feet up on an imaginary dividing wall. "This room to the left will be the parlor, and over here . . . " he led her into the room to the right of the staircase, "is the dining room. We'll have a beautiful view of the river."

Elizabeth smiled. "*We*? Don't you mean *they*—the new owners when we sell?" Despite her correction, she couldn't help thinking like Jacob, that the place was really their own.

Jacob simply shrugged and led her toward the back of

the house, past the centrally located chimney, stopping just the other side of the stone structure. "And this, my darling, is the kitchen. I had Uncle Will lay an especially wide hearth for cooking, and there's plenty of space for cupboards. The pantry is right here." He stepped around a couple of sawhorses to a generous space at the very back.

The kitchen was no small affair, and Elizabeth could already envision the rag rug Louisa was making, spread out beneath the table from their cabin for informal meals. Taking the basket from her arm, she rested it on one of the sawhorses. "I'm ready to eat my first meal in our new house. Too bad there's no table."

Will leaped into the kitchen through the unsided back wall. "We can fix that." He rearranged the sawhorses. "There. Now, all we need is a few boards from the scrap pile."

A minute later, he and Jacob had erected the makeshift table, and while Elizabeth spread out her picnic lunch, the men hammered together a bench. Will set it in place, adjusting it for a fine view of the river, then eagerly partook of the cornbread and smoked whitefish Elizabeth offered him. He finished quickly, then strolled down to the river, leaving Elizabeth and Jacob alone.

As Elizabeth munched on her cornbread, she contemplated the view of the river, the forested lots either side of the new house, and the peaceful atmosphere interrupted occasionally by the buzz of a locust or the chirp of a sparrow. Despite the crudeness of the Saginaw Valley, she was beginning to appreciate the tranquility Riverton offered.

Jacob studied the pretty woman by his side, silently pleased that she had shown such interest in the progress on the house despite initial objections. He set aside his napkin and took her hand in his.

"You know what I think, Elizabeth?" he said contemplatively, "I think you're starting to like our house and our river—just a little bit."

She offered a smile. "It certainly looks different from the canal back home." Putting napkins and cups into her basket, she said, "Now, I think it's time for me to go home and let you get back to work. I'll see you at dinner time."

Several days later, when Elizabeth set out by canoe with Jacob and Will for the business meeting the men would attend in Upper Saginaw, the mid-August weather proved hot and sultry. She was thankful for the coolness of the river, and dampened her handkerchief in it to wipe the perspiration from her face.

When Jacob and Will turned their canoe toward shore near Pierce's Mercantile, Elizabeth noticed that someone else had already pulled a canoe up on the riverbank. Coming closer, she recognized it as the one belonging to Beloved-of-the-Forest and Walks Tall, so it was no surprise that when she, Jacob, Will, and Louisa entered the general store, the Indian couple was inside, bartering with Mrs. Pierce. Three deer skins lay on the counter, and beside them, an iron kettle and two frying pans.

"These are lovely," Mrs. Pierce said, inspecting the hides. "Very fine. But not worth what you're asking." She put the two frying pans aside. "I'll give you the kettle for them."

Beloved-of-the-Forest spoke quietly with Walks Tall, then turned again to Mrs. Pierce. Putting one hand on the deerskin and the other on the kettle, she said, "One for one."

"Oh, no! *Three* for one," Mrs. Pierce insisted.

Out of earshot of Mrs. Pierce, Elizabeth heard Will tell Louisa, "I've seen Chippewas get three for one in Detroit, only there, it was three pans for one hide."

Speaking in quiet tones to Will, Elizabeth said, "It's a shame the Chippewas should get such a poor deal from Mrs. Pierce when they could do so much better in Detroit. Isn't there some way we could help them?"

"What about Capt'n Winthrop?" Louisa asked. "He could take them—I mean those—hides on the *Governor Marcy*."

"And Beloved-of-the-Forest's baskets, too," Elizabeth added. "Mrs. Pierce won't take them in trade, even though they're superior to the ones she's already selling."

Jacob joined the conversation. "I don't know about Captain Winthrop. He's mighty shrewd. By the time he took his cut, Beloved-of-the-Forest and her husband might not be any better off trading in Detroit than they are right here."

Their conversation paused while Walks Tall and Beloved-of-the-Forest passed by on their way out of the store with the one kettle Mrs. Pierce had agreed to give in trade. When the door had swung shut behind them, Elizabeth said, "I suppose you're right, Jacob. We can't expect Captain Winthrop to be of any help, knowing firsthand the premium he's getting for passage on his boat."

Though Elizabeth disliked Mrs. Pierce and her high prices, she purchased an embroidery hoop and needle, colored floss, and a length of linen to make into a baby quilt. At the hotel, she checked into the room she'd be sharing with several other women.

At six, she went with Jacob, Will, and Louisa to the

dining room. It was filled to capacity for a meal of pork roast with all the trimmings, and wild blackberry pie. Dinner seemed to stretch on for hours, and Elizabeth was glad when the men adjourned to the tap room for their business meeting and she could go upstairs to get her handiwork. She was pausing to gaze out the window that overlooked the alley behind the establishment and the forest beyond, enjoying the cool evening breeze, when she saw Brother-of-the-Wolf come in off a wilderness trail. He was carrying two large, gutted fish.

Mr. Otis, the hotel proprietor, stepped outside, inspected the fish Brother-of-the-Wolf had brought, then held the door while the Indian carried them inside. When the Chippewa reappeared, he was holding a whiskey flask, and Elizabeth watched in shock and disappointment as he twisted off the top and took a long drink of the liquor.

"Brother-of-the-Wolf, no!" she shouted out her window.

He paused to look up, and evidently not seeing her, went back to his drinking.

She hurried out of her room and down the stairs so fast, she nearly tripped. Catching her balance, she rushed out the front door and around back. Brother-of-the-Wolf was only yards ahead of her on the forest trail.

"Brother-of-the-Wolf, stop!" she shouted, hurrying after him.

When he recognized her, he set his flask behind a tree and turned to face her. "Greetings, Medicine Lady," he said without expression.

"Brother-of-the-Wolf, don't do it! Don't drink whiskey!" she pleaded, going straight to the hidden flask.

As she reached for the whiskey, he grabbed her painfully by the wrist and forced her aside. "Go away! Brother-of-the-Wolf need strong drink!"

"No you don't!" Elizabeth argued. "What about Father God? He can help you! He can take away your need for alcohol! You told me you walk with Him now. Are you giving up your new faith so soon?"

Brother-of-the-Wolf crossed his arms on his chest and looked her squarely in the eye. "Old spirit, Gitchie Manitou, no like new spirit, Father God. Old spirit make big trouble. Brother-of-the-Wolf walk no more with Father God."

"But Father God can help you in any kind of trouble," Elizabeth insisted.

"Father God weak." Abruptly, he turned away, taking his flask with him down the trail.

Elizabeth couldn't resist calling after him, "Maybe it's Brother-of-the-Wolf who's weak, did you ever think of that?"

Deeply disappointed, she returned to the hotel, but the vision of Brother-of-the-Wolf tipping whiskey to his lips haunted her for the rest of the evening, and into the night when she sat alone in the lobby, waiting for Jacob to come out of his meeting.

CHAPTER

7

Jacob tucked away the cigar his uncle had given him, pushed aside the whiskey Mr. Otis had poured despite his polite refusal of strong drink, and sat back to listen to what the eighteen men who had converged on the tap room at the Upper Saginaw Hotel had to say, thankful that at least some of them--Mr. Farrell, Captain Langton, and Mr. Sayers—were familiar to him. The Upper Saginaw men had proven themselves quite outspoken at the dinner table, and they continued to dominate the discussion now.

"What we need up here is roads!" Pierce claimed from the opposite side of the large, round table. "What good is a general store when nobody can get there, 'cept by canoe?" He drew on his cigar and emitted a series of smoke rings into the already hazy, foul-smelling air.

"What we *need*, Pierce, is livestock," argued James Cromwell. "Ya cain't build roads without oxen, and ya cain't do much farmin' without some hefty work horses."

"You're right, Cromwell," said Fred Fenmore. "We need to clear more land and plant more crops. Ain't nobody gonna make use of roads, or a store, 'less they got crops to sell."

"You fellas got it all backward." Isreal Stevens, owner of the Upper Saginaw Mill, shook the gold head of his cane at the others. "What we need first is a bigger mill. My mill is gonna open up this forest for all the rest of you—for your roads, Mr. Pierce, your livestock, Mr. Cromwell, and your farmland, Mr. Fenmore."

The others grumbled.

Will rose and tapped his empty glass on the table. "Gentlemen, gentlemen, if I may." When the room quieted, he continued. "You're overlooking the obvious. There's only one way we're going to get the roads Mr. Pierce wants, the livestock Mr. Cromwell suggests, the farmland Mr. Fenmore recommends, and the expansion for the mill Mr. Stevens operates. It's called money. We need a bank. And we can establish one ourselves—right here in Upper Saginaw if you want—and issue our own bank notes. Once people have money, there'll be no stopping the progress here in the Saginaw Valley."

"How can we put up a bank?" Pierce challenged. "There's not much gold or silver around. I ought to know. Most everything going out of my store is on barter."

"Hard cash is mighty scarce," Isreal Stephens pointed out. "When those folks from your home state of New York put out that specie circular, everybody started hording it."

"Yeah, Morgan. Tell us how y'r gonna have a bank without hard cash?" Henry Otis asked as he refilled Will's glass.

"And without a lot more investors than we've got here," Isreal Stephens put in.

"Last things first," said Will confidently. "We only need twelve men who own land in the county to be the investors. We've got more than that right here, right now."

"So what do we have to do?" Captain Langton asked.

"As investors, you put up your land as collateral for loans to purchase shares in the bank. Then, you pledge the

90

stocks for the loans you received to buy them."

"You sure that's legal?" James Cromwell wanted to know.

"Absolutely," Will responded.

"But we've still got hardly any gold or silver," Mr. Pierce reminded him. "How are we going to back bank notes without hard cash?"

"There's a simple answer for that," Will replied. "In June, Governor Mason relieved all the Michigan banks of the requirement to pay out gold and silver in exchange for their notes. As for finding enough gold to start up our own bank, I've got connections. I can *guarantee* we'll have enough. The most important thing right now is to find a way to make the Saginaw Valley grow."

"Yeah! With more than just pine trees!" said Fenmore.

Will continued. "Back in York State, when Clinton's Ditch was being dug, villages prospered by the establishment of new banks to give entrepreneurs credit. After a while, everybody was much better off. That's how my brother and I got started in the banking business twenty years ago. There's no reason why we can't make the same plan work here in the Saginaw Valley!"

Jacob listened as the men near him began to speculate about the wealth and prosperity sure to come to Upper Saginaw and Riverton with the opening of a bank. Soon, their attention was on him.

"The way your uncle explains it, it's a simple thing, setting up a bank," Mr. Farrell commented.

"You're a banker. Is it really such a sure thing?" Mr. Sayers wanted to know.

Jacob considered the question carefully. "My father and brother still run the bank Papa and Uncle Will started, and it's doing very well. I suppose, with the tightening of the money supply, things are a little different now. But my uncle has more experience than I do. If he says a bank can make Upper Saginaw and Riverton successful, there's a good chance he's right."

As the others talked among themselves, Jacob pondered one question his uncle hadn't clearly answered. Excusing himself from the table, he drew his uncle away from the Upper Saginaw men who were seeking answers to questions of their own.

"What is it, Jacob?" Will asked, his hazel eyes gleaming with excitement. When Jacob hesitated, he grew impatient. "Out with it, nephew. These fellows from Upper Saginaw are warming up real nice to my ideas. I don't want them to go cold."

"Uncle Will, there's something I'm not sure I understand," Jacob began. "You said you could get enough gold to start a bank, but you never explained your connections. I'd like to know just how you *are* going to get the hard cash you need?"

Will drew a deep breath. "Jacob, I know folks in other towns this side of Michigan who have the same problem we do in the Saginaw Valley—no money circulating to build their communities. We've discussed what's needed for the banking inspector, and we've come up with—shall we say a cooperative method—of pleasing him. Now excuse me. I've got to bring this meeting back to order so we can make some definite plans to get this bank started."

Moments later, when everyone's attention was again on Will, he said, "Like I told you at the start, we need twelve landholders to establish a bank. Men in other towns have done it—places like Flint, Grand Rapids, Marshall, Battle

Creek, Jackson, and several more. We can organize like they did."

"So far, all I've heard is the good side," Captain Langton said. "What do we stand to lose if our bank fails?"

"Yeah, what if it goes under?" Mr. Sayers echoed the captain's concern.

"Good point, gentlemen. Certainly there are risks, but before I explain them, let me emphasize, they're minimal. As for the stockholders of the bank, they will be personally liable for an amount equal to the stock they hold. In order to start up, we have to make a deposit with the auditor of mortgages on land in Michigan, or personal bonds equal to the indebtedness of the bank."

Captain Langton spoke again. "So if I pledge my land for stock in the bank, and the bank goes bust, I've got no land."

"There's little chance of that. It's only paper!" Will said. "I'll work hard to make the bank succeed. I'll go to Detroit and recruit settlers to come here. It will be easy when they know our towns have everything they need to thrive, including a bank! Now, let's have a vote to see how many of you are ready to take the next step to make our county grow. All those in favor of chartering the Saginaw Valley Bank, raise your hands."

Jacob noticed that Pierce, Cromwell, Fenmore, Stevens, Otis, and one other from Upper Saginaw raised their hands along with his uncle. Five more stockholders would be needed. Though Jacob wanted to support his uncle, he was suspicious that some irregularity would be involved.

"Come on, gentlemen," Will prodded. "You don't want to languish here on the shores of the Saginaw River while other towns around prosper, do you?"

In the undercurrent that followed, three more gentlemen raised their hands—Mr. Farrell, Mr. Sayers, and one other.

"That's ten. We need two more investors—two men with a vision for the future of the Saginaw Valley. Captain Langton, what about you?"

The captain rose, his gaze taking in the entire company. "I spent twenty-five years risking my life at sea, saving up so I could retire on solid ground." Focusing on Will, he continued. "The land you sold me at a premium price is pretty nearly all I've got. I'm not about to risk it." The room was silent except for the sound of the captain's boot heels as he headed for the door.

An Upper Saginaw man by the name of Patterson stood up. "Bankin's not for me either, Mr. Morgan."

"Nor me," said his friend, a fellow known to Jacob only by the name of 'Turtle.'

When they had made their exit, Pierce spoke up. "Don't pay them any mind. Langton may have been brave at the helm of his ship, but he hasn't got enough heart to put the good of the Saginaw Valley ahead of his fears. We only need two more men willing to do the right thing and put up some land. Who's got just a little courage? McLaughlin? What about you?"

"It's not for me," the gray-haired fellow told him. "Like the captain, I'm too old." He headed for the door.

"Harper, you're not too old," Pierce said, his attention on a strapping fellow in his thirties with a dark beard and mustache.

Harper finished off a shot of whiskey and set the glass on the table with a clunk. "All right. I'm in. But you'd best not breathe a word to my wife. We got five younguns, and she gets unbearable angry if she thinks I've gambled even one penny in a card game. She won't take to me puttin' up a piece of our land for a bank. Not even if the chance of losin' it was only the size of a fly's eye."

Jacob was keenly aware that besides himself, only two brothers by the name of Nichols remained undeclared on the bank question. The elder Nichols rose to speak. "Mr. Morgan, my brother 'n I respect what y'r tryin' to do here, but we just can't be a part of it."

As they headed out the door, the focus of eleven men turned to Jacob. Pierce offered him a wry smile. "Looks like this bank needs one more Morgan."

"My nephew will pledge land," Will said confidently, "won't you, Jacob?"

He realized now that this was what lay behind Will's gift of the ten parcels either side of his lot.

"Come on, Morgan," Pierce cajoled.

"Yeah, Morgan. Come on. Don't ya trust your own uncle?" Cromwell gibed.

"It's gettin' mighty late," Fenmore grumbled. "I'd sure like to get this settled. Now how 'bout it, Morgan?"

Jacob rose and addressed the party. "All right. I'll put up some land—under one condition." Speaking with great conviction, he continued. "Uncle Will, you and the others have got to promise me you'll run the bank strictly by regular banking practices."

"Of course, nephew! Strictly by regular practices."

"Here, here!" Pierce cheered. "To the Saginaw Valley Bank, run strictly by regular banking practices!"

"Here, here!" chimed in Otis, pouring out more whiskey.

"Three cheers for the Saginaw Valley Bank!" said Cromwell.

When the cheers had died down, Fenmore said, "Once we get ourselves the bank, this wilderness 'll change in a hurry. Then maybe I'll sell my land, make lots of money, and move farther west!"

Will Morgan grinned broadly. "Maybe we *all* will, Fenmore! Now, let's call to order the first meeting of the directors of the Saginaw Valley Bank. We've got to write up the articles of our incorporation. The sooner we get started, the sooner we can file them with the auditor in Detroit. Then, I can go to New York City and get our bank notes printed up by the engraver. Within weeks, we'll be in business!"

CHAPTER

8

Jacob left the tap room at the break of dawn, too exhausted to think of anything but dragging himself upstairs to the room he was sharing with five other men. But as he passed through the hotel lobby, he found Elizabeth asleep on a bare wooden bench.

"Elizabeth, wake up," he said softly, kneeling beside her and jostling her shoulder.

She murmured something unintelligible, her eyes blinking open. Coming wider awake, she lifted her head. "Jacob, what time is it?"

"A little before six."

"You've been up all night?"

He nodded. "It's a long story. Are you awake enough to hear it?"

She pushed up to a sitting position and Jacob sat beside her, his arm about her. Laying her head against his shoulder, she asked, "What's Uncle Will up to now? It must be something big, to keep you in a meeting all night long."

Jacob shared the details of the plan to establish the bank, and his own reluctant involvement. Then, he explained Will's newest idea. "He's planning to go to Detroit to file the articles of incorporation for the bank with the auditor, then on to New York City to hire an engraver to print the bank notes. He wants me to go to Detroit with him to see if we can both sell some land. He says he'll even pay passage for me *and* you on the *Governor Marcy!*"

"Well, glory be!" she said with surprise, sitting up straight to face him.

Jacob chuckled. "You'll like another suggestion he had, too."

"What's that?"

In a more serious tone, he said, "You should take some of those Chippewa baskets and hides, and have Beloved-of-the-Forest make up some moccasins, and see what you can get for them in the city."

Elizabeth took Jacob's hand in hers. "Darling, that's a wonderful idea. I'd be so pleased if I could make a good trade for Beloved-of-the-Forest and Walks Tall." Suddenly overcome by a yawn, she said, "I think we should both go upstairs now, and try to get some rest. Then, if you're willing, we could go to the worship service in the lobby after breakfast. The men folk around these parts take turns reading from the Bible and leading prayer. It won't be the same as Reverend Clarke's sermons, but we could pray for God's guidance where the bank and the trip are concerned."

Jacob pulled Elizabeth close beside him. "You know what I think, Elizabeth? I think you are a very wise woman, and we should go upstairs just as soon as I've given you a kiss."

Two hours in a room with five other women—three of them snoring—kept Elizabeth awake despite her fatigue. But when she rose and noticed that Louisa was no longer in the bed, she realized she must have fallen asleep, for she hadn't heard her friend leave.

Jacob was waiting for Elizabeth downstairs when she reached the lobby, dark lines beneath his eyes betraying his own lack of rest, but his smile was handsome, nevertheless.

Taking her by the hand, he said, "Come to the dining room. Will and Louisa are waiting for us, and they say they have something important to tell us."

Jacob seated her across from Louisa on the bench near the end of a long, pine table. Ten other hungry guests had already started eating breakfast, leaving an empty platter. But Mrs. Otis appeared promptly with a fresh supply of flapjacks, syrup, bacon, and coffee, and soon everyone's plate and cup was filled.

"I'd like to ask the blessing," said Uncle Will, joining hands with Louisa and Elizabeth. When Jacob had done the same, Will continued, head bowed. "Dear Heavenly Father, we thank you for this bountiful meal you have set before us, and ask your blessing on the marriage into which Louisa and I will soon enter. In Jesus' name, Amen."

"Marriage?" Elizabeth asked with delight.

"When is the wedding?" Jacob wanted to know.

"Saturday, if Reverend Clarke agrees," Louisa answered, her face beaming.

"Of course, if the *Governor Marcy* comes along and Captain Winthrop decides to depart for Detroit before week's end, we'll have to get married even quicker," Will explained, "but I don't expect that will be the case."

"We'll have at least a few days to prepare, then," Elizabeth concluded.

"No fuss needed, bein' this is my second weddin'," Louisa told her.

"*Some* fuss is in order," Will argued amicably. "After all, I'm getting hitched for the very first time, and I've come up with some plans. First, I'm renting Fenmore's mare for you to ride. No horse has ever come to Riverton before. His bay mare will be a right pretty sight, prancing around town with you on her back."

"You needn't go to the trouble," Louisa told him. "I don't much like horses."

"You'll like Fenmore's," Will insisted. "She's the sweetest, gentlest thing you ever did see. And we're going to need her to start out the procession."

"A procession to where?" Elizabeth wondered.

"From the village down to the river," Will replied.

"I can walk that far in a couple of minutes," Louisa informed him, "but if it'll make ya happy to have a horse, then I guess ya got a right. After all, it *is* the first wedding for Riverton." She smiled at Will affectionately.

"And it will be the first opportunity for the Chippewas to see how we white folks take one wife at a time in a proper, Christian ceremony," Will pointed out. To Jacob and Elizabeth, he explained, "We're inviting all the Indians from the Chippewa village for the wedding, and a feast afterward."

Elizabeth shuddered, remembering her encounter the previous night with Brother-of-the-Wolf. "You won't have any strong drink at the feast, will you, Uncle Will? Because I saw Brother-of-the-Wolf out back of the hotel last night trading fish to Mr. Otis for a flask of whiskey."

Color invaded Will's cheeks, and his fist came down on the table. "Why, that red-skinned scoundrel! He's not setting one foot in my town if he's back to his old, bad habit!" A silent, angry moment passed, then Will spoke again, his good humor restored. "I'm going to barter for that hog Langton's been fattening up so we can all have some fresh roast pig at the wedding feast. Elizabeth, I'm putting you in charge of the cake. After morning services, I'm going across the street and prevail on Mrs. Pierce to open up and sell me a cone of white sugar and a sack of white flour, even if this *is* Sunday. You and the other ladies can make us a fine white layer cake, can't you?"

"We'll do our best," she promised.

An hour later, while Mr. Otis was leading the opening prayer in the church service, Elizabeth couldn't help thinking how hypocritical he sounded. He prayed for the success of Reverend Clark in bringing the civilizing influence of the Christian religion to the Chippewas, yet he himself was guilty of supplying Brother-of-the-Wolf with the demon whiskey.

Judge not, lest ye be judged. The Biblical warning sounded in Elizabeth's head. She quickly asked forgiveness for her sin, then prayed that Mr. Otis would find some other method of barter for the fish the Chippewas brought him. Nevertheless, she had to struggle to keep her mind on the Bible lesson he preached from Jeremiah, "Ask, and I will answer."

He had closed his Bible and asked Mr. Cromwell to say the final prayer when she heard a faint sound from outside the hotel. Someone near her whispered, "The *Governor Marcy's* comin'." She listened carefully, then heard the unmistakable, *toot, toooot* of the vessel's steam whistle.

"Amen!" said Cromwell, mid-sentence.

"Amen!" the congregation echoed. Everyone scrambled to their feet, abuzz with excitement.

"Come on. I've got to go talk to Captain Winthrop," Will said, taking Louisa by the hand and making haste for the door. "We might be holding that wedding celebration sooner than we thought!"

Elizabeth and Louisa waited on the riverbank with

Jacob while Will climbed aboard the boat to confer with Captain Winthrop. When Mr. Pierce showed up in search of the supplies he'd ordered for his mercantile, Jacob prevailed on him to open the store long enough to sell him the sugar and flour for the wedding cake. They were still at the store when Will came ashore, beaming from ear to ear.

"Captain Winthrop demanded an invitation to the wedding next Saturday in exchange for letting me book passage to Detroit," he announced to Louisa and Elizabeth. "He's even going to bring wedding guests from Upper Saginaw down to Riverton at no charge, and depart for Detroit immediately following the feast!"

"How perfect!" Louisa cried happily.

"It's going to be the best day ever!" Will boasted, throwing his arms about her in a big bear hug that lifted her off her feet.

"Put me down this instant, you joker!" Louisa demanded.

He set her down, then gazed about. "Where's Jacob?"

"He's gone after the sugar and flour," Elizabeth explained.

Reaching into an inside pocket, Will pulled out several letters. "Captain Winthrop gave me the mail for Riverton. There's a letter for him from his father." Thumbing through the other missives, he paused to study the face of an envelope. "Here's one for you, too, Elizabeth. From someone by the name of Knight, postmarked three weeks ago in Buffalo."

"I don't know anyone in Buffalo by that name," she said. Reading the envelope, the handwriting seemed vaguely familiar. She turned it over and loosened the wax seal, then took out the two-page letter and looked immediately for the signature at the bottom—Sallie Simmons Knight. "Sallie Simmons! Aunt Sallie!" Elizabeth murmured in disbelief.

"A letter from your aunt?" Louisa asked politely.

"An aunt I haven't seen or heard from in years," Elizabeth explained, her heartbeat quickening. "Excuse me, won't you?" She started toward the privacy of the oak tree a few yards downstream.

"Louisa and I are going up to the store to find Jacob while you catch up on news from Buffalo," Will said, heading for the mercantile hand in hand with his intended.

Elizabeth leaned against the old tree and with shaky hands, began to read.

> July 21, 1837
> Dear Elizabeth,
>
> You must be wondering why, after so many years of silence, I am writing to you now. I won't keep you guessing. I am on my way to Michigan with my family. When we stopped in Brockport to tell you and your father that we are moving West, imagine my surprise when he informed us you had already taken up residence in Michigan!
>
> It eases my mind greatly to know someone familiar is already living in the state I will soon adopt as my new home. Your father has given us to believe there is still plenty of land for sale in Riverton. My husband seems amenable to locating there, and we expect to arrive sometime within the month or as soon as we can arrange passage out of Buffalo. As you already know, the wait can be lengthy.
>
> There is much more to tell, but I will leave it until

we see one another, except to say that I am married to Isaac Knight, a blacksmith by trade. We have two sons by his first marriage. Todd is thirteen and Charles is twelve. We also have two daughters of our own. Amy is already six, and Sarah just turned five. Now I must close and post this with the hope it reaches you before we do.

Affectionately, Aunt Sallie

Elizabeth read the letter several more times wishing it revealed some explanation for Sallie's sudden disappearance from her life so many years ago. Old nigglings of guilt stirred within. Though Elizabeth had not been able to think of any way in which she had offended her aunt, she had always blamed herself for Sallie's mysterious departure. The question regarding her leaving would have to wait until they were reunited and she could ask it face to face.

Tucking the letter into her skirt pocket, Elizabeth pondered the almost unbelievable news that her beloved aunt wanted to take up residence in Riverton. It pulled Elizabeth's heart in two directions at once, wanting to return to Brockport in the fall, yet not wishing to leave Sallie, who would have so recently settled in. She put those thoughts aside when she saw that Louisa, Jacob, and Will were coming toward her, arms laden with packages. Louisa's face was flushed with excitement.

"You're not gonna believe the things this man just bought at the mercantile! Piece goods and fancy lace trims for me. New boots and a brand new hat for himself!"

"Nothing's too good for our wedding day, dear. It's the one day above all others, we want to look nice," Will said, handing a package to Elizabeth. "For you, niece. Make yourself a new dress and bonnet for Saturday. You'll stand up for Louisa, won't you? Jacob already said he'll be my witness."

"Thank you, Uncle Will," she said, accepting the parcel. "I'd be pleased to serve as Louisa's matron of honor."

Pulling his letter from his pocket, Jacob offered it to Elizabeth. "You'll want to read this. Papa sends news of Mama and Henry, and your father, too. Uncle Will says you've received a letter from Buffalo. Was it from someone we met on our way to Michigan?"

Elizabeth shook her head. "No. It's from a relative of mine, Aunt Sallie. She's the one who took care of me for a time after Mama died."

Jacob scratched his chin. "Was she at our wedding?"

"No. I would have invited her, but I didn't know where to send her invitation. Now she's written to say she's heading for Michigan. She's got a husband and four children, and they're planning to settle in Riverton. She's married to a blacksmith."

"A blacksmith! Well, bust my buttons!" Will slapped his thigh. "Riverton sure could use a blacksmith. Jacob and I could stand to sell off some land, too. What's the name of your aunt's husband?"

"Knight. Isaac Knight."

"Let's see. That letter of yours was canceled by the Buffalo Post Office three weeks ago. I'm guessing the Knights will get to Detroit about the time we do. Jacob, you and I are going to find them and offer Mr. Knight such a deal on Riverton land, he'll be writing his York State friends about it the very same day!"

Elizabeth shook her finger at Will. "Just don't tell them

there's a town with stores and churches and frame houses and that the lots are already cleared."

"Now would I do that?" Will asked, a mischievous gleam in his eye.

Despite her distrust, Elizabeth chuckled.

Putting his arm about Louisa's waist, Will said, "Come, dear. It's time to head home. I need to meet with Reverend Clarke today, if possible, and settle our wedding plans." To Elizabeth, he said, "I'm looking forward to that cake you and the ladies are going to bake. Just think of it! A real layer cake! When was the last time you had that?"

"At my own wedding, as I recall," Elizabeth replied, wondering how she would manage to bake a cake without an oven, a recipe, or any experience. She would visit Mrs. Langton later today and seek her help with the task.

Later on, as the Riverton dock became visible from the canoe, Jacob paused in his paddling and strained for a clearer view. "Uncle Will, it looks like there's a broken barrel on your dock."

Will shaded his eyes with his hand. "Sure looks that way." As the canoe came alongside the pier, he saw that the door to his blockhouse had been split apart, and inside, kegs, casks, and firkins lay strewn about. "Looks like Brother-of-the-Wolf's been up to his old tricks again!" he said angrily. "I'm going over to that village right now and tan his hide so hard, he won't sit down for a month!"

"It doesn't seem to me Brother-of-the-Wolf would break open a barrel of salt pork," Jacob observed.

Will grew livid. "Don't defend that scoundrel!" he warned. "I'm going to the Chippewa village right now and have it out with him!"

CHAPTER

9

While Jacob helped his uncle clean up the mess on the dock and in the blockhouse, Elizabeth carried home the staples for the wedding cake and the piece goods Uncle Will had given her. When she had opened the windows to air out the cabin, she set off for Mrs. Langton's with the white flour and sugar.

A curious sight caught her eye outside the Langtons' cabin. The fence around their pigpen had been broken, and the hog Uncle Will had planned to roast for his wedding feast was nowhere in sight.

Elizabeth pulled the Langtons' latchstring and stepped into the cabin. Clara was stirring a pot over the fire at the back of the cabin while Jane and Ruth worked salt into slabs of meat on the table. A repugnant odor filled the air.

Jane greeted her first. "Mrs. Morgan, come on in. We're making salt pork."

"A bear killed papa's hog last night, and we had to butcher it," Ruth explained.

"Did you say a bear killed your hog?" Elizabeth asked.

"That's right," said Clara, setting aside her spoon. "I heard a real ruckus early this morning before the captain came home from Upper Saginaw. An ornery old bear was trying to carry off the pig. I tried to shoot the big old critter, but my aim wasn't too good. At least he dropped the porker before he ran off. But by then, the pig's neck was broken, so we had to slaughter it right away."

"Papa said he saw a bear trying to get into the block-house this morning when he was on his way home," Ruth said.

"Mama thinks it was the same one that killed our pig," said Jane.

"We both noticed a big notch in the fellow's right ear," Clara explained. "The captain scared the fellow off, but I suppose he'll come again."

"He already has!" Elizabeth exclaimed, setting down the flour and sugar and heading for the door. "I'll be back shortly. I've got to go tell Uncle Will what you've just told me."

As swiftly as her legs could carry her, she hurried toward the blockhouse, encountering Jacob at the top of the steps to the dock. "Where's your uncle?"

"He's taken his gun and gone to the Chippewa village to see Brother-of-the-Wolf."

"You've got to stop him!" Elizabeth insisted. "Captain Langton saw a bear trying to get into the blockhouse this morning. He scared him off, but the captain figured he'd return."

"That explains the fresh bear tracks I found next to the dock." Jacob headed for the trail. "I've got catch up with Uncle Will before he makes trouble at the Indian village!"

Will Morgan fumed all the way to the Indian village. Brother-of-the-Wolf had already cost him plenty since he'd bought land and settled in the Saginaw Valley. All winter long, the Indian had stolen from his traps, claiming he'd set them on the line his tribe had used for years. Couldn't that

Chippewa get it through his thick skull that his people didn't own the forest anymore? Will Morgan had bought and paid for it, and it was all legal in the eyes of the United States Government and the new State of Michigan.

Instead of accepting Will as a new neighbor, Brother-of-the-Wolf had become downright hostile, and a menace to the peaceful white settlement. His breaking down the cabin door and ruining nearly everything Elizabeth and Jacob had brought to Riverton was one costly incident Will wouldn't soon forget. It had been a mighty expensive proposition for him and the other Riverton folks, making things right for Elizabeth and Jacob so they wouldn't turn around and head back to Brockport almost as soon as they'd arrived. At Brother Clarke's urging, Will had refrained from going to the chief to ask recompense for damages done by the young brave. The reverend had insisted that Brother-of-the-Wolf had truly changed, becoming a Christian and giving up strong drink.

Obviously, the conversion didn't *take*. The Chippewa had already reverted to his old drinking habits and violent rages.

"No more!" he grumbled to himself as he strode along the path to the Indian camp. "Will Morgan is done being generous and forgiving!"

As he marched into the Chippewa village, his rifle propped on his shoulder, he paid little heed to the young braves outside their huts, playing their games of chance in the dirt. The odor of smoked fish filled the air as a Chippewa woman hung whitefish fillets over a rack to dry. The stench of wild game boiling in a pot came to him as he passed another hut where squirrel was being cooked, hair and all.

Up ahead, three wolf dogs lay in the dust outside the deerskin door to Brother-of-the-Wolf's wigwam. When Will stopped in front of the hut, they growled softly and bared their teeth. He lowered his gun from his shoulder, and loaded it with a powder charge.

"Brother-of-the-Wolf! Come out!" Will demanded loudly.

Braves from the neighboring hut paused in their dice game. From inside Brother-of-the-Wolf's hut, Will heard a moan, and some jumbled words in Chippewa.

"I said, come out!" Will repeated. Setting his rifle into his shoulder, he aimed at a cloud and set off the powder charge.

The dogs scrambled to their feet and began to bark and growl menacingly. Will loaded his rifle with a round this time, ready to protect his own hide against the four-footed beasts if necessary.

"Brother-of-the-Wolf, come out and answer for your deeds!" Will demanded again.

Slowly, the hide was lifted from the hut door. Crouched in the semi-darkness of the wigwam was Brother-of-the-Wolf, his hair disheveled, his expression a portrait of misery, his dark eyes opening only a slit as he squinted out at Will. Issuing a subtle command, his dogs grew quiet, and laid down.

"I do no wrong," Brother-of-the-Wolf told Will.

"You've probably forgotten what you did last night when you were drunk," Will insisted, "but you're going to pay for your mischief!"

The Indian retreated behind the deerhide door.

Will shook his fist at Brother-of- the-Wolf's hut, then set off to find the chief at the longhouse at the center of the village. Chief Noc-chick-o-my was a fair man. He would understand Brother-of-the-Wolf's transgressions, agree to pay for them, and find a way to prevent them in the future, or there would be big trouble between the white man and the Chippewa.

Will propped his rifle against the building and lifted the skin at the narrow end of the longhouse, ducking to enter. Despite the dim light, he could see the chief sitting on a bearskin at the opposite end of the hut, legs crossed. Beside him was Reverend Clarke, reading from a Chippewa Bible.

The minister set the Holy Book aside and offered a smile when he saw Will. "Brother Morgan, what brings you to the Chippewa village today?"

Will answered grimly, "Trouble, that's what. Brother-of-the-Wolf got drunk last night and went on another rampage. I'm here to strike a deal with the Chief for damages to my barrel of salt pork and the door to my blockhouse."

"Please come and sit," Reverend Clarke suggested.

As he settled on a grass mat facing the chief, the clergyman translated Will's words. Moments later, Reverend Clarke interpreted the chief's response.

"Chief Noc-chick-o-my asks what proof you have of Brother-of-the-Wolf's guilt. Did you see him break the door of the warehouse or damage the barrel of salt pork?"

"Everybody knows I was down to Upper Saginaw for the night, including Brother-of-the-Wolf," Will answered in frustration, "but there's no doubt about the time he busted into my nephew's cabin. This is just another example of the same."

Reverend Clarke entered a discussion with the chief. A

few minutes later, he translated for Will. "Chief Noc-chick-o-my doesn't think Brother-of-the-Wolf is to blame for the damage last night, but he's sorry for your loss. He'll have Brother-of-the-Wolf deliver a basket of dried whitefish to you tomorrow, to store for winter. The corn crop has been sparse this year, and the Indians won't have any to share with the white folks, as they did the last two winters."

"A basket of whitefish?" Will fumed, on the verge of refusing the gift. Then he thought better of it. "You tell the chief I expect no more trouble from Brother-of-the-Wolf, or I'll have it out with that young man!" He headed out of the longhouse and down the path toward Riverton. Minutes, later, he noticed Jacob running toward him.

"Uncle Will . . . " he paused to catch his breath, "have you already been to see Brother-of-the-Wolf?"

"You bet your last barrel of salt pork, I have! But he was in no condition for conversation, so I had a chat with the Chief. He's giving me a basket of dried whitefish so I won't go hungry this winter. Imagine that!"

Still breathing heavily, Jacob said, "Brother-of-the-Wolf . . . wasn't to blame . . . this time."

Will set the butt of his rifle on the ground with a thump. "Who, then?"

Quickly, Jacob explained about the Langtons, and the fresh bear tracks near the blockhouse. "The Chief's people had nothing to do with this trouble. We've got to go back and tell him the truth."

Will grinned. "We'll do no such thing." He turned away, keenly aware that Jacob wasn't following him.

As Jacob watched him go, thoughts spun through his head—about Will's exaggeration of Riverton when selling him his lot; about his description of the LaMore place as a comfortable honeymoon cabin. Jacob had long ago forgiven his uncle for his lies, but he wasn't about to allow deceit where the Chippewa were concerned. Running to catch up, he jumped on Will's back, taking him down to the ground.

Will hit the dirt hard, his rifle falling from his grip and firing accidentally. When he picked his face up out of the dust, Jacob was standing in front of him feet apart, rifle beneath his arm.

"I can't let you do it, Uncle Will. I can't let you make me a party to your deception. We're going back to the Chief and tell the truth." He pointed the rifle in the direction of the Indian camp.

Will stood and brushed off the dust. "All right, Jacob. I'll go back to the Chief," he said with resignation, "but for goodness sake, be careful with that rifle."

Reverend Clarke and the Chief were still in conference when Will entered the longhouse with his nephew. "Sorry to interrupt again, but Jacob and I have some news that can't wait," Will explained, taking his place on the grass mat. Jacob sat beside him. "Reverend, tell Chief Nocchick-o-my that I come to ask his forgiveness. My nephew has learned that a bear did the damage to my blockhouse and barrel of pork, not Brother-of-the-Wolf."

A moment later, the reverend explained Chief Nocchick-o-my's response. "He forgives you, and asks that you accept the fish anyway. He says hunger in winter is the worst kind of hunger, and he doesn't want his neighbors to suffer."

A corner of Will's mouth curled upward. "Tell the Chief I accept his gift on one condition. You must officiate at a wedding for me and the Widow Tyler this coming Saturday, and the Chief and his people must attend both the wedding ceremony and the dinner afterward."

The clergyman offered a wide smile. "Congratulations, Brother Morgan! I'll be honored to conduct the service." Following an explanation in Chippewa that brought a nod from the Chief and several words in his guttural language, the minister said, "The Chief accepts your invitation on behalf of his people, and offers to supply squirrel stew and fried bread."

Will wanted to refuse, but he knew better than to cast an insult now that relations with the Chief were smooth again. "Squirrel stew and fried bread sound mighty tasty," he said, hoping Louisa would understand the modifications to the wedding menu.

Excitement stirred within Elizabeth, waking her early on Saturday morning. Thoughts of the wedding and the trip to Detroit afterward to trade baskets, moccasins, and hides for Beloved-of-the-Forest and Walks Tall wouldn't let sleep return, so she arose sooner than she had wanted. Following a breakfast of blackberry pancakes and bacon with Jacob, she sat with him over a cup of sassafras tea.

Jacob pushed aside his teacup, reaching for the hand of the woman who had become dearer to him with each passing day in the Michigan wilderness, and more precious because of the child she carried. Coming around the table, he drew her to her feet and took her gently in his arms. "You know, I'm really proud of the way you've learned to get on here in Riverton."

Elizabeth couldn't help noticing how muscular Jacob had grown over the summer, and in his eyes shown a look of devotion that had deepened with each passing week. Aside from his more caring, tender ways, she was highly pleased with the progress he had made on the house. The clapboard he had recently put on gave it a substantial, attractive appearance.

"I'm proud of you, too, Jacob. You came to Michigan a banker, and look at you—you're a successful builder! It should be easy to find someone to buy our house."

Jacob tried to smile, but couldn't. For weeks, he had secretly hoped Elizabeth would find the house so appealing, she'd want to stay. She had certainly shown plenty of interest in it, coming once a day or more to check on the progress. "Perhaps we will," he said half-heartedly.

Elizabeth didn't miss the flicker of disappointment in Jacob's blue eyes, nor his lack of conviction when he spoke of selling. For days she had been contemplating her changing feelings about the house and Riverton, the satisfaction she gained from teaching the girls of the community, and the news that her aunt was en route to this very town. Now was the perfect time to share her new thoughts about the future.

"Jacob," she took his face gently in her hands, "when we go to Detroit, promise me one thing."

He remained silent. He was certain Elizabeth would request that he do his best to sell their property and get their investment back while they were in Detroit.

A smile crept across Elizabeth's face. "Promise me you won't sell our house."

Jacob gave his head a shake, certain his hearing was faulty. "Did you say you *don't* want me to sell the house?"

She nodded vigorously.

"Elizabeth!" He hugged her tight, lifting her right off

the floor. "I haven't felt this happy since our wedding day!" He set her down to kiss her.

"Jacob?"

He took her hands in his. "Yes, darling?"

"I still want to go to Brockport for the winter to have the baby. But as soon as the ice melts, we can come back. I know you'd prefer to stay in Michigan, but—"

"Elizabeth, if you want to keep the house, you'll have to go East without me. It's the only way to protect both our baby, and our investment."

"No . . . " she said, unconvinced. "There has to be another way."

Jacob squeezed her hands. "You and the baby need your papa. As for the house, we've got too much invested to leave it for the winter."

"We could get someone else to stay there while we're gone. The Clarkes!" Elizabeth suggested.

Jacob shook his head. "They haven't announced it yet, but they're going East on furlough for the winter."

"Then what about the Langtons, or the Farrels?"

"I know there are others who would be happy to move in for a few months, but I won't allow it," Jacob insisted. "I won't have others occupying the brand new house I built for my wife before she even gets a chance to live there!"

Elizabeth's heart was filled with so much love for Jacob, she couldn't argue. "If only Papa were going to be *here* when the baby arrives," she lamented.

"Don't fret, darling. Everything will be fine." He kissed her on the forehead. "I'm heading down to the riverbank now, and make sure all is ready for the wedding. And I'll see if Walks Tall and Beloved-of-the-Forest have brought their trade goods to load onto the *Governor*

Marcy."

"Would you please carry these to our table?" Elizabeth asked, indicating the place settings for her and Jacob, and a canister of biscuits she'd baked for the feast.

"Certainly." He tucked the canister beneath his arm. "Now, why don't you get dressed for the wedding while I'm gone. I'll be back and get cleaned up in a while."

Thankful for the private time for her morning ablutions, Elizabeth put thoughts of the pending separation aside while she washed up, brushed her hair and fastened it in a knot, then slipped into the new dressed she'd made. Despite the attractiveness of the pretty cotton print Uncle Will had bought her, she couldn't help thinking how casual this wedding would be in comparison to her own formal nuptials two months ago in Brockport. Then, silk and lace had been the order of the day.

She fingered the ruffles Louisa had shown her how to make from white cotton for the large collar that trimmed her blue calico dress. In Brockport, a seamstress had sewed every stitch of Elizabeth's gown and those of her bridal attendants. Here, in Riverton, Louisa had made her own dress, and helped Elizabeth extensively with hers, and a bonnet to match. Even so, Elizabeth had needed help from her students in order to finish in time. She was thankful that Clara Langton had taken complete responsibility for baking the cake. At least Elizabeth hadn't wasted a minute worrying about that, she thought, as she picked up her mirror to inspect the results of her sewing efforts.

Though she could see only partial images of herself in the small glass, she was pleased with the outcome. The sleeves, puffy at the shoulders and narrow from elbow to wrist, brought the latest fashion even to these remote parts of the Saginaw Valley, and the gathers above the waist masked the fact that she was expecting.

Jacob returned to find her staring in the mirror, tying a bow in her bonnet strings. "Mrs. Morgan, you look lovely indeed." He came up behind her and kissed her neck.

Chills went through her, as they always did when he caressed her there, and she shuddered, despite the warmth of the day. "How was everything at the river?" she asked, offering a brief hug, then spreading a towel on the table and setting out his shaving supplies.

"The trade goods are ready to be loaded," he replied, reluctantly sitting down to tackle the stubble on his cheeks and chin. With a laugh, he added, "And Mrs. Langton is keeping guard over her cake."

While Jacob made himself ready, Elizabeth went into the woods to pick wild roses to tuck beneath the brim of her bonnet. When she returned, he was wearing a muslin shirt with a red print scarf for a tie.

Elizabeth chuckled quietly. "I was just thinking how folks in Brockport would talk if they could see how informal Will and Louisa's wedding party is dressed."

"They wouldn't see any waistcoats and doublets, that's for certain," Jacob assured her. "Uncle Will's planning to wear a buckskin jacket and—" Jacob stopped mid-sentence, listening to the sound of a distant whistle. "That's the *Governor Marcy* coming in with the guests from Upper Saginaw. Come on. Uncle Will's probably looking for us."

Elizabeth slipped her arm in Jacob's, briskly covering the distance to the riverbank. Mr. Otis, Captain Winthrop, and several others from the neighboring town were already gathered around Will and his rented bay mare. When Elizabeth saw the bridegroom, she thought he looked the epitome of a frontiersman, attired in a fringed buckskin jacket and breeches, and sporting a brand new Bowie knife that hung in a sheath at his waist.

Will positioned himself and the horse on the path to Louisa's. "It's time to fetch my bride! Captain Winthrop, Mr. Otis, strike up the music, if you please!"

Mr. Otis put his harmonica to his lips, Captain Winthrop tucked his fiddle beneath his chin, and a happy tune filled the air along the trail. When they reached the Tyler cabin, Louisa was standing outside her door, and Elizabeth couldn't help noticing she had never looked prettier. Her white poke bonnet was lined with pink roses that matched both her dress, and the blush in her cheeks. Will picked her up and put her on the barebacked mare as if she were as light as a rag doll.

Mr. Otis raised a flask. "To the prettiest bride in the Saginaw Valley!"

Elizabeth caught the momentary look of disapproval on Will's face before his smile reappeared. "More music, Mr. Otis!"

The flask disappeared into Otis's pocket and cheerful notes rang out again. The merry company continued past the other cabins until all the Riverton folks had joined the parade. When they reached the north end of the village, the Chippewas were waiting in a long line on the riverbank path, and fell in step behind the others.

Within minutes, the entire assembly gathered about the altar where Reverend Clarke, Mrs. Clarke, and little Jeremy Tyler were waiting. Speaking in Chippewa, the clergyman invited Chief Noc-chick-o-my and his two wives and children to stand beside him, then he began.

119

"We are gathered together . . . "

In clear tones, Mrs. Clarke translated the entire ceremony into Chippewa for the Indian guests. At the end, when Will kissed Louisa, murmurs of approval went up from the Chief.

"Ho, ho. Ho, ho," he said, almost smiling.

Will turned to face his guests. "Let the wedding feast begin!" he proclaimed. Beaming with pride, he took Louisa in one hand, the reins of the horse in the other, and led them the short distance to the head table, stepping in time to Captain Winthrop's fancy fiddling.

As Elizabeth helped dish out squirrel stew and roast venison, she saw a curious sight. Mr. Otis was talking with Brother-of-the-Wolf beneath a tall pine at the edge of the forest. Otis offered the Indian a drink from his flask. Brother-of-the-Wolf refused. Elizabeth was offering up a silent prayer of thanks for Brother-of-the-Wolf's abstinence when she caught sight of Beloved-of-the-Forest serving dinner at a table a few yards away. The Chippewa woman was wearing a beautiful red cotton shift. Intricate patterns had been stitched into it with colored threads and beads. The same design was carried out on the red cotton headband the Indian wore. Elizabeth hurried to greet her friend.

"Beloved-of-the-Forest, you look lovely!"

She lowered her gaze self-consciously. "You like?"

"Very much!" Elizabeth assured her.

Beloved-of-the-Forest smiled openly, and without further words, returned to her work, serving the guests at her table.

When everyone had eaten their fill of stew, venison, fried bread, and the other dishes passed at the feast, Clara Langton carried a three-layer cake decorated with white frosting to the table of the bridal party. Elizabeth thought how much the woman seemed like the Pied Piper of Hamlin, coming across the clearing with a string of children following at her heels. Quickly, Elizabeth moved aside Louisa's and Will's dishes to make a place for the slightly lopsided, but highly tempting confection.

Carefully, Clara set it before the newly married couple. "You'd best cut it now, before one of these anxious younguns gets a fingerfull of frostin'," she told Louisa and Will.

"I've got just the knife," said Will, unsheathing his Bowie knife.

"I shoulda known ya couldn't settle for any ordinary knife to cut y'r weddin' cake," Louisa teased. She was about to take the Bowie knife in hand when a tremendous growl sounded from the north edge of the woods.

Elizabeth turned to find a monstrous black bear charging out of the forest on a direct path for the cake!

CHAPTER

10

"Run!" Jacob shouted, grabbing Elizabeth by the hand.

The others took off in several directions, but she couldn't make her feet move.

Fear coursing through him, Jacob swept Elizabeth into his arms just as the bear crashed into the table. He headed for the blockhouse as swiftly as possible. Descending the riverbank steps, he glanced back over his shoulder. The bear was several yards behind, closing fast.

Onto the dock Jacob ran, nearly falling when his toe caught against an uneven plank. Somehow, he managed to keep hold of Elizabeth, catch his balance, and carry her inside the blockhouse.

"Climb up to the loft!" he ordered, pushing her in the direction of the ladder. When he turned to close the door, the bear stood just inside the threshold, rearing up, pawing the air. His angry growl reverberated against the wooden walls.

Jacob scrambled for the ladder, discovering Elizabeth stalled at the top rung.

"There's no room for us in the loft!" she cried.

"Hold tight to the ladder!" Jacob warned, climbing up as far as he could.

The bear reached the ladder, grunting and growling. Rising up on his hind feet again, he swiped at Jacob's legs.

"Go away! Get out!" Jacob hollered, kicking hard at a menacing paw.

The bear put his front paws against the ladder and began to shake it. The bottom rung dropped to the floor.

"Hold tight, Elizabeth!" Jacob warned, searching for a way to distract the animal. A stack of kegs stood to the left of ladder. Reaching out, he pushed with all his might. The highest keg fell to the floor. As it rolled toward the door, the animal dropped down on all fours to follow it.

"Stay where you are, Elizabeth," Jacob ordered, stepping onto the kegs that remained.

Evidently dissatisfied with his toy, the bear turned his attention on Jacob once more. Rising up, he let out a mighty roar, then crashed into the stack of kegs that remained, bringing them down, and Jacob with them. He scrambled to his feet and backed away from the bear, keeping two kegs between them.

The huge creature lunged, pushing aside one keg, then the other.

Jacob backed up against the wall. The bear swung his huge paw. Jacob shielded his face with his arm. The blow never came.

A loud, guttural cry went up. Jacob opened his eyes to discover Will with his Bowie knife thrust into the bear's back.

The bear howled again in anger and pain.

Will withdrew his knife. The bear turned on him. Will took a stance, preparing to stab the beast again.

With a swipe of his paw, the bear knocked the knife from Will's hand, fell on him, and began to maul him.

Jacob grabbed the knife. With a two-handed grip, he brought it down hard, aiming for the bear's kidney.

The animal bellowed louder this time. He tried to get up. Will scrambled from beneath and backed away, then fell backward over a toppled keg. The bear crawled toward him.

A blood-curdling scream rent the air as Brother-of-the-Wolf leaped forward. He thrust his own knife into the bear's gut. The animal swiped at Brother-of-the-Wolf, gouging his face.

Jacob pulled the Bowie knife from the bear's back and stabbed him again and again. Brother-of-the-Wolf slit its throat. The animal fell on the blockhouse floor. A silent moment followed, broken by a trembling female voice.

"Jacob!"

At the sound of his name, Jacob turned to find Elizabeth shakily descending the ladder. "Careful! The bottom rung is missing!" he warned, hurrying to set her on the ground.

She wrapped her arms about his neck. "Oh, Jacob, I've never been so frightened in all my life!"

Hugging her tighter than ever before, Jacob half-whispered, "Neither have I, my darling." A long moment later, he reluctantly released her.

"Are you two all right?" Will asked, pressing a hand-kerchief to a bleeding scratch on his neck.

Jacob massaged his left shoulder. "Just some bumps and bruises." Taking Elizabeth's hand in his, he added, "And one severe case of fright. How about you?"

"I'll be fine."

Several Indians entered the blockhouse and began to help Brother-of-the-Wolf haul the dead bear away.

"Brother-of-the-Wolf, thanks!" Jacob called.

"Yes, thanks!" said Will.

The Indian nodded. Ignoring the blood trickling down his face and neck, he concentrated on carrying off his prize.

"Thank God, he got here in time," Jacob said reverently.

"And he wasn't drunk," Will pointed out.

"I saw him refuse a drink from Mr. Otis's flask just before the wedding dinner began," Elizabeth said.

"Looks like I'll have to have another talk with Otis," Will said. "I've told him before not to trade whiskey with—"

He stopped abruptly when Brother-of-the-Wolf entered the blockhouse. Holding the Bowie knife handle out, he returned it to Will.

"Thanks," Will said, tucking the knife into its sheath. When Brother-of-the-Wolf turned to go, he called after him. "Wait up. I want to talk to you."

Brother-of-the-Wolf paused just outside the door. On the riverbank several yards beyond the dock, his people were butchering the bear. Facing the Indian, Will looked deep in his dark eyes. The Indian returned his gaze unwaveringly.

Will spoke thoughtfully. "Today, Brother-of-the-Wolf drank no whiskey. Today, Brother-of-the-Wolf killed mighty bear. Today, Brother-of-the-Wolf is hero among white men and Chippewas. Now, tell me. Tonight, will Brother-of-the-Wolf drink whiskey? Tonight, will Brother-of-the-Wolf be drunk and weak?"

Several moments passed. Finally, the Chippewa walked away, leaving Will wondering whether the Indian had truly understood his questions. Jacob interrupted his thought.

"That's some new knife you've got."

Will drew it from his sheath. The bright sun glistened off the blade. "When I traded yesterday for this Arkansas toothpick, I had no idea it would help save my life today," he mused.

"That's God's grace. Divine timing," Elizabeth concluded.

"Perhaps so," Will replied. From the corner of his eye, he caught sight of movement atop the riverbank, and turned to find Otis headed for the Indians.

"Otis, I want to talk to you!" Will hollered, hurrying toward the other man.

When he caught up to him, the hotel owner grinned. "You'll have some story to tell your children and grandchildren about the bear that came to your wedding feast, Morgan."

Will scowled. "And you just thought you'd come down and see if the Chippewas are willing to trade that bear meat for some whiskey."

Otis put his hands up, palms out. "No, no. I told you last time we talked, I wouldn't give the Indians any more alcohol, and I meant it."

"You lied!" Will said angrily. "You offered Brother-of-the-Wolf a drink from your flask. Elizabeth saw you."

Smiling nervously, Otis shrugged. "What's one drink? One innocent little swallow never hurt anybody."

Will stepped up, face to face with Otis. "You know full well it only takes a taste to get a Chippewa drunk. You broke your promise to me. You're off the board of directors for the Saginaw Valley Bank!"

"We'll see about that!" Otis challenged. "It takes

twelve to start a bank. Who you gonna get to replace me?"

"Somebody who knows right from wrong where the Indians are concerned. Now get out of here!"

After the excitement of the wedding feast, Jacob was thankful for a few minutes of quiet, alone in the cramped cabin on the steamer. The warm weather, together with the heat from the boilers down below, was keeping Elizabeth up on deck in the fresh air this evening. While she lingered in the company of Will and Louisa, he stole a few minutes to get out his pen, ink, writing paper, and two envelopes.

Weeks had passed since he'd written to his folks in Brockport. He'd been too busy building the house, and too tired when he wasn't working on it, to actually set words to paper.

After he had written and sealed his first letter, he took pen in hand again and started a second one, giving serious thought to its wording. He needed to be persuasive, but honest about Michigan, and Riverton in particular. With a silent prayer for inspiration, he let the ink flow. When he had finished his appeal, he tucked the missive away where Elizabeth wouldn't find it. Though it held no startling revelations, he felt it best to keep the letter a secret until a reply was forthcoming.

Finished with correspondence, Jacob emerged from the cabin. Orders from the Captain were being relayed to the boiler room to put on more wood. Jacob worried that Winthrop was pushing too hard to take advantage of the relative calm on the lake and make time on the run. He'd heard often enough of boilers fired too hot and exploding. As the pulse of the engine picked up, he climbed to the deck and studied the smokestack. Dusk was settling in, making the sparks from the stack appear like harmless little fireflies escaping a black cloud. He prayed it was so, and when the *Governor Marcy* had passed safely to Detroit, he gave thanks.

With a sense of futility, Jacob approached the dock in Detroit where the passengers from the *Ohio* were about to debark. He'd met the steamer *Michigan* and the schooner *Erie* earlier that afternoon, and had spent the morning checking registers at the hotels and inquiring among the crowd of emigrants outside the Detroit land office. Thus far, no one had heard of Isaac Knight from Genesee County, New York, the husband of Elizabeth's Aunt Sallie.

Jacob paused to take off his hat, pull his already soaked handkerchief from his pocket, and mop the sweat from his brow. The day was uncomfortably hot, humid, and still, enhancing the stench of horse excrement built up from the heavy traffic of drays along the riverfront. Jacob wanted nothing more than to return to the hotel and treat Elizabeth and himself to some cold lemonade—if any ice was to be found in the city—but he couldn't risk the chance that her kin would be coming off this boat.

He approached the first middle-aged male passenger to step off the *Ohio*, holding little hope that this slightly built individual was a blacksmith. But the family with him—a woman with two boys and two younger girls—fit the description in Aunt Sallie's letter. Half-heartedly, Jacob stepped up to the man.

"Sir, I'm looking for Isaac Knight. Do you know if he was aboard?"

The fellow's broad smile engulfed a considerable portion of his long, thin face. "That, he was. But he's stand-

ing on the dock talking to a perfect stranger right now."
His hand shot out. "I'm Isaac Knight. And you're . . . ?"

"Jacob Morgan." The man's firm grip belied his spare
frame, proving he did indeed possess the strength of a
blacksmith.

His wife stepped forward, and Jacob realized that she
was actually taller than her husband by a good two inches.
"Did you say Morgan?" Her brown eyes, reminiscent of
Elizabeth's, focused anxiously on Jacob.

"Yes, ma'am. I'm married to your niece, Elizabeth
Brownell, of Brockport. She's back at the Woodworth
Hotel, and she's going to be mighty pleased I've found
you!" Turning to the young ones, he said, "Now let me
guess. These must be Todd, Charles, Amy, and Sarah, if I
remember your letter correctly."

"Right, you are," said Isaac. "Children, say hello to Mr.
Morgan."

When each had greeted Jacob in turn, he spoke again to
their father. "All the hotels are full up, but you're welcome
to share our room at the Woodworth. My uncle, Will
Morgan, will be returning there later. Either one of us can
sell you parcels of land in Riverton for your smithy and
your new home. In a few days, the *Governor Marcy* will
take us up there."

"I'm anxious to meet your uncle, and your wife," said
Isaac, "but first, I'd better make sure our belongings are
properly handled."

"I can help you with that," Jacob offered. "Captain
Winthrop is already expecting you aboard for his next trip
north."

"No need to trouble yourself," said Isaac. "If you'll just
wait here with my wife and children, I'll make the neces-

sary arrangements with our Captain Holcomb."

"Louisa, they're here!" Elizabeth cried, looking out her second story window as Jacob, her Aunt Sallie, and the rest of the Knight family approached the Woodworth Hotel. She had spent nearly the entire day watching for them, and had nearly given up hope. The only interruption in her tiresome vigil had been when the dray had delivered the Indian baskets, hides, and moccasins from the *Governor Marcy*. But at last her relatives were here! Picking up a paper cone of lemon drops she had purchased that morning, she headed for the door.

"Don't ya want these, too?" Louisa asked, holding up the candy canes Elizabeth had bought out of sheer boredom earlier in the afternoon.

"Yes, bring them. And come quickly!" She hurried down the stairs so fast, she nearly tripped. Grabbing the handrail to catch her balance, she spilled the cone of lemon drops which bounced down the remaining steps and into the lobby jammed with emigrants from out East.

Instantly, several children scooped up the sweets. Disgusted with herself, Elizabeth crushed the paper cone into a ball, dropped it into the wastebasket at the bottom of the stairs, and rushed out onto the plank sidewalk.

She paused at her first glimpse of her aunt. The woman had a much more severe look than Elizabeth remembered, with her hair pulled back and her bonnet tied tight beneath her chin.

"Aunt Sallie!" Elizabeth rushed ahead.

The wide smile that greeted her was instantly familiar, washing away the years that had come between, and softening the apprehensive expression into one of warmth and congeniality.

"Elizabeth, I never would have recognized you! My, but you're a beautiful bride!"

Though her aunt's embrace added warmth to an already unbearably hot day, Elizabeth was reluctant to let go.

Sallie squeezed her tight before releasing her. "Elizabeth, meet my daughters, Amy and Sarah, and my stepsons, Todd and Charles."

"My pleasure." Elizabeth shook each of their hands in turn, noting that the girls had inherited blond hair and blue eyes from their father, while the boys must have come by their taffy-colored hair from their mother.

Louisa stepped forward. "Elizabeth, you had somethin' special for these young kin of yours, didn't ya?" She held up the candy canes.

"I nearly forgot! Aunt Sallie, is it all right if I give each of your children a peppermint stick? It's my token of welcome to Michigan."

"Please, Ma?" Amy and Sarah begged almost in unison.

"All right, but only if you promise you'll clean your plates at supper. It's getting late in the afternoon for sweets."

"We promise!" the girls chorused.

When all four of the children had thanked Elizabeth for their treats, Jacob said, "Elizabeth, every hotel in Detroit is full up, so I've invited the Knights to share our room until the *Governor Marcy* goes north. Let's take them up there now, so they can wash up. Uncle Will should be back soon, then we can all go to dinner together."

Elizabeth linked her arm with Sallie's. "Come on, I'll show you our quarters." Starting toward the hotel, she said, "I still can't believe you're actually here!"

As Jacob listened to his wife talk excitedly with her long lost relative, he said a silent prayer of thanks that he had been able to locate the Knights. Later, at dinner, when conversation turned to the Knights' recent visit to Brockport, he noticed that Elizabeth listened carefully to her aunt's every word.

"I didn't know what to expect," Sallie told her, "not having seen your papa in so many years. He's looking extremely well— except for that forlorn look in his eye when he admits he misses you."

Elizabeth's gaze dropped momentarily, hinting at a touch of homesickness.

Isaac took up the conversation next. "Much as I liked your father, I must say, I found him a bit boastful. He went on at great length about the fact that you helped to save the Indians from smallpox. That's when I tried to convince him to move to the Saginaw Valley. I said we needed the assurance of having a well-seasoned medical team to call on. He grew a little quiet then, and I actually thought he was considering it. Then he told me this moving-west fever didn't seem to infect older folks, just us younger ones, and as far as he knew, the only cure for it was the one we're taking—up and moving bag and baggage."

As the conversation moved on to other topics, Jacob prayed silently again, this time for the special letter he'd written, that his words would produce the intended results when delivered to York State by Uncle Will.

The topic turned then from medicine to land and the price of Michigan real estate. When everyone had finished their piece of custard pie, Uncle Will said, "Nephew, it's time we took Mr. Knight across the street to the tavern and rolled out that map of Riverton so he can decide where he wants to put up his smithy and his house." Mopping the perspiration from his forehead, he added, "Besides, with this weather, I could do with some refreshment."

When the dinner tab had been paid, Will paused in the crowded lobby to dig loose change from his pocket. Placing several coins in his wife's hand, he said, "Louisa, see that you and Elizabeth and Mr. Knight's kin have all the lemonade you can drink. We'll be back in a while to take you for an evening stroll."

"We'll prob'ly be out on the porch waitin' for ya," said Louisa. "It's a good sight cooler there than inside."

"I'd like to go up to the room first for a minute, if you don't mind," said Sallie. "Children, come along."

At noises of objection from the young ones, Louisa said, "You go on up, Mrs. Knight. I'll take the children outside for some fresh air, if it's all right."

"Thank you kindly, Mrs. Morgan." To the children, she said, "Behave yourselves. Boys, watch out for your sisters, and don't tease, you hear?"

"Yes, ma'am," said Todd and Charles.

Elizabeth dabbed the perspiration from her forehead. "I'll go upstairs with Aunt Sallie, Louisa. We won't be long."

"No need to hurry. This is a lazy night, if I ever saw one," said Louisa, taking Amy and Sarah by the hand.

Upstairs, Elizabeth dampened her handkerchief in the pitcher of wash water, laid it against her forehead, and leaned back on the bed. While Sallie sponged off her own face, neck, and wrists, Elizabeth couldn't stop wondering about the one question that had plagued her since her aunt's sudden disappearance from her life so many years ago in Brockport.

With a sigh, her aunt sat down beside her, still mopping away the moisture with a towel. Sensing the rarity of these moments alone with Sallie, Elizabeth sat up, gazing directly into her aunt's brown eyes, and spoke bluntly. "Tell me something, Aunt Sallie. Why did you leave Papa and me?"

Sallie fidgeted with the towel, then stood again. "I . . . I can't say." She dipped the corner of the towel into the wash water and wiped her face, turning her back to Elizabeth.

"Can't, or won't?" Elizabeth gently challenged. "I've asked myself a hundred times what I did to make you go away. To this day, I carry guilt over it."

Sallie whirled around. "Oh, but you mustn't!"

"Then tell me why you left. *Please,*" Elizabeth pleaded.

"It was your papa," she quickly replied. "We had a falling out."

"You and Papa?" Elizabeth asked, incredulous. "But I never heard a cross word between you!" After a moment's further consideration, she continued. "Aunt Sallie, after you left us, Papa's Cousin Agatha came to stay with us. She and I argued nearly every day, and Papa didn't fare much better. I saw Papa angry enough to send someone away, and I know that wasn't it with you. Won't you please tell me what made you go?"

Sallie shook out her towel and hung it on the bar of the washstand. "I'm sorry, Elizabeth. I haven't anything more to say on the matter. Now, I must go downstairs and see to my children."

CHAPTER

11

The moment Will stepped into the noisy tavern, he was sure the place was packed with potential customers for his land. They were jammed elbow to elbow along the bar, and all the tables were full, as well. The smell of pipe smoke enhanced by the profound essence of body odor permeated the atmosphere, and the air was filled with the noisy boastings and braggings of a rough brand of men.

"Uncle Will, maybe we should go up to our room," Jacob suggested.

Will shook his head. "This is the place where deals are made. We might find more customers for our land. I can get us a table. Just you watch."

He walked up to a table of four men he didn't know, placed a Spanish bit on it, and easily persuaded the fellows to do their imbibing on their feet. Pressing his way to the bar, he placed his order with the tavern wench, and within minutes, a pitcher of ale and three mugs were delivered to the table.

Will poured ale all around, then unrolled his map. "Mr. Knight, I've been saving a choice parcel of land on Main Street for your smithy—right on the corner of River Avenue. You'll be but a stone's throw from the waterfront. Everybody heading to the dock will pass by your shop." He pointed to the lot platted on the map.

Isaac studied the diagram a moment, then took a pair of eyeglasses from his pocket and looked at it again. Will realized that in the dim light, the property lines were not easily visible, but the blacksmith pored over the chart without complaint.

When no comment was forthcoming, Will continued. "This lot is thirty feet wide by fifty feet deep. There's more land available either side. I'll give you a more favorable price if you buy the three lots together."

At that moment, a huge man stepped forward, and Will found himself staring into the craggy face of the one person he'd hoped never in his life to see again.

"Quigley." The name nearly stuck in his throat.

"It's been three years, Morgan." He tapped his wide index finger on the map. "How much you askin' for that dime-sized lot?"

Will offered a cold stare. "That's between me and Mr. Knight. Now move along, Quigley. You've got a bad habit of shoving in where you're not wanted."

Quigley took a swig from his mug, then wiped his overgrown beard and mustache on his muslin shirt. "You haven't seen the last of me yet, Morgan. We've got unfinished business."

Will rose, his face inches from Quigley's. "Our business was finished long ago, when I bought the Riverton section. Now be on your way." An uneasy moment followed, then Quigley wandered off.

Will sat again. "Sorry, for the interruption, Mr. Knight. Now where were we?"

Isaac resumed his study of the map, pointing to the lot Will had recommended. "How much *are* you asking for this lot, Mr. Morgan?"

"For prime real estate like that, fifty dollars."

Isaac drew a quick breath. "For one small lot? But you couldn't have paid more than a dollar and a quarter per acre for that land."

"That was when it was just forest. Now it's been improved. It's a town. The town of Riverton. See the streets and the park—"

"Uncle Will," Jacob cut in, "be honest. The streets, the park, and even the lot Mr. Knight is considering are *still* just forest."

Will glared at his nephew.

"You mean this land you're trying to sell me hasn't been improved yet?" Isaac wanted to know.

Will sighed. "No, Mr. Knight. You'd have to take down a tree or two, but I'm more than willing to help you with that. We'd have it cleared in no time, then you could get right to work putting up your smithy."

Isaac put away his eyeglasses and focused on Will. "Mr. Morgan, to tell you the truth, I'm not sure I want to move any farther than I already have. I've noticed, just in the distance from the dock to this hotel, that Detroit is growing so fast, there's going to be plenty of work right here for another blacksmith."

Quigley stepped up to the table again, plunked his mug on the center of the map, then rested his hand on Isaac's shoulder. "Couldn't help overhearin' you're a smith. I know a smithy could use a man of skill, startin' tomorrow. Pays real good, too."

Will rose. "I warned you to keep your distance. Now, be on your way!" He shoved Quigley's mug into his gut.

Anger flashed in Quigley's eyes. With a quick upward movement, he pushed Will away, spilling his mug's contents on the map and sending the cup tumbling onto the floor.

Will raised his fist. Before he could take a swing, Jacob sprang from his seat, wedging between him and Quigley.

"Back off, Uncle Will!"

A moment later, Will lowered his fist.

"That's better, Morgan. Now don't try pullin' no fancy deals here." Quigley picked up his mug and turned away.

"Let's go up to our room," Jacob suggested again.

Will nodded, mopping the spill from his map. He was a bit surprised to discover it wasn't ale, but lemonade. Perhaps Quigley had changed some in the last three years.

On the way back to the hotel, Jacob paused on the porch to promise Elizabeth he would be back soon to take her for a stroll. By the time he reached the room, Will was unrolling his map on the center of the only bed. His uncle drew up the room's one chair for Isaac Knight to sit on, then sat on the end of the bed while Jacob took a seat on the floor.

"Mr. Knight," Will began, "before we left the tavern, you were entertaining the possibility of living in Detroit. I want you to think what it would be like, settling here. Property has gone sky-high. Besides, the city is crowded, dirty, and overrun with traffic. Is this any way to live?"

Isaac thought a moment. "Just what do you have in Riverton, Mr. Morgan? Jacob says it's still forest, but you show a church on your map. Do you have a church?"

Will answered reluctantly. "No, but we've got a preacher—a missionary to the Indians. He holds services for us white folks, too."

Isaac pointed to the schoolhouse on the map. "I suppose you haven't built a school yet, either."

"No. But we've got a teacher—Jacob's wife is schooling the girls right in her cabin."

"What about my boys?"

"We'll be putting up a schoolhouse real soon, I'm sure," Will insisted.

Indicating the lot marked 'General Store' on Will's map, Isaac asked, "Is this business in operation yet?"

"Not exactly," Will admitted.

"Now just what does that mean? Is it under construction?"

"Not yet. I intend to start on it real soon. In the meantime, my blockhouse is full of supplies. If you need something, I'll sell it to you. If I don't have what you need, there's Pierce's Mercantile in Upper Saginaw. That's four miles from Riverton."

Isaac pondered the situation. When a few moments had passed, Will spoke again. "Mr. Knight, think what Riverton has to offer. You can raise your family in a quiet little community. You'll know everyone in town. Land is reasonable enough so that you can buy plenty for yourself, and your sons, too.

"And there's lots of work waiting for an ambitious smith up there. Jacob and I have had a real tough time just getting enough nails to put up his house. We've had to make a trip to the smithy in Upper Saginaw at least once a week. Sometimes we have to stay all day to make sure the hammerman finishes our order. Otherwise, he takes on other jobs and puts ours aside."

Isaac nodded thoughtfully. "How many people actually live in your community right now, Mr. Morgan?"

"We're small, but—"

"How many?" Isaac pressed.

Will shrugged. "Haven't made an exact count lately. With newcomers moving in all the time, it's hard to keep track."

Jacob spoke up. "Half a dozen families live in Riverton, Mr. Knight. They're good, God-fearing folks. Most of them hail from York State, like you."

Isaac drew a deep breath and let it out slowly as he put away his eyeglasses. "To be honest, I've heard western Michigan is the place to go. Some folks who came across Lake Erie with us on the *Ohio* are going to settle on the Grand River."

Jacob spoke again. "I don't wish to sound out of turn, Mr. Knight, but Elizabeth is your wife's kin, and I'm given to believe Mrs. Knight is eager to be our neighbor." After a moment's pause, he added, "And your belongings are aboard the *Governor Marcy*."

Isaac shook his head. "Captain Holcomb agreed to hold them one night so I could make a decision which direction to take from here. And Sallie will live where I say." Isaac rose from his chair, paced slowly toward the door, then back again. "You do have a valid point, though, Jacob. Sallie would be disappointed if she couldn't live near Elizabeth." Turning to Will, he said, "But I won't pay fifty dollars for one lot."

After some haggling, Isaac set several gold pieces on the map in front of Will. "Take it or leave it. That's my final offer."

Will scooped up the gold coins. "Sold!"

Isaac turned to Jacob. "I'm hoping you'll sell me two lots for a house just north of the one you're building." He pointed to the plots on the map, and made an offer.

Jacob's hand shot out. "It's a deal!"

"Those are fine choices you've made," said Will. "Now that you're a landowner in the Saginaw Valley, I have a proposition for you. How would you like to be on the board of directors of my bank?"

"I don't see any bank marked on the map," Isaac observed.

"That's because I haven't built it yet," Will explained. "I'm about to file incorporation papers, but I do need one more director, and you're just the man to fill the spot!"

While Will and Isaac discussed details of the bank, Jacob went down to the porch. The Knight boys appeared restless and bored, but the girls' smiles were a welcome relief from the serious business of land sales.

Amy jumped up from her place on the front step and grabbed hold of his hand. "Cousin Jacob, will you take us for a walk now?"

Sarah claimed his other hand. "*Please* take us for a walk. We've been waiting a *long* time!"

"If your mother and your Aunt Elizabeth say it's all right, we'll all go for a walk now," Jacob told the girls.

"I'd be much obliged if you'd take us, Jacob," said Sallie.

"So would I," said Elizabeth. Reaching down to touch Todd's shoulder, she said, "Seeing as how my husband is occupied with your sisters, would you be my escort?"

"Yes, ma'am," he replied timidly, offering his arm.

"Then maybe Charles could walk between his mother and me," said Louisa. "He seems growed up enough to have a lady on each arm."

Charles sprang to his feet. "It'd be my pleasure,

ma'am."

"Which way shall we go, girls?" Jacob asked.

"That way!" Amy and Sarah replied in unison, pointing in opposite directions.

"There's a candy shop to the right," said Elizabeth.

"To the right, it is," said Jacob, stepping off the porch. They had gone only a few yards when Sarah pointed across the street.

"Look! A spotted puppy!" Breaking free, she ran toward it, directly into the path of a fast-moving wagon.

"Sarah, watch out!" Jacob shouted, bolting after her.

She stumbled and fell. The wagon bore down on them, forcing Jacob to step back. When it had rattled past, he saw that Sarah was safe on the other side in the arms of Quigley. The hefty man set Sarah gently on the wooden walk, keeping hold of her hand.

"You saved Sarah's life!" Jacob exclaimed.

"This your daughter?" Quigley asked.

Jacob shook his head. "She's my wife's cousin."

Sarah tried to pull free from Quigley. "Let me go, mister! I want to see the puppy!" She tugged hard in the direction of the black and white dog.

"Hold on, little miss. We can't have you running in the road again." He gave a sharp whistle, and the puppy bounded over. "Sarah, meet Rascal."

"Rascal!" She was kneeling down to hug him when the others came running across the street.

"Sarah! Shame on you! You know better than to run in the street!" She scooped her daughter up. Focusing on Quigley, she said, "How can I ever thank you, Mr. . . "

"Quigley's the name."

Sarah wiggled in her mother's arms. "Put me down,

Mama. I want to pet Rascal."

Sallie set her daughter down, holding her securely by one hand while she pet the dog.

Elizabeth, Louisa, Amy, and the boys joined them, and when introductions had been made, Jacob told Quigley, "Mrs. Knight's husband was the blacksmith with my uncle and me when you saw us in the tavern. They're moving to Riverton."

"So you're the ones buying land from Will Morgan," Quigley concluded. "I know his holdings well. Seems to me, you oughta have a puppy up there in the Saginaw Valley. Your child's welcome to take Rascal along."

"Mama, can we, *please?*" Sarah begged.

Sallie shook her head. "You're kind to offer, sir, but we have no place to keep him until the *Governor Marcy* goes north."

"Her," Quigley corrected. "Rascal's a female spaniel. I'll be glad to keep her till the boat heads north."

Todd spoke up. "Please let us have the dog, Mama. I really miss Yorker." To Quigley, he said, "Papa had to put our dog down when we left New York. We'd had him as long as I can remember, and Mama said he was just too old to make the trip."

"I'll take care of Rascal just like I did Yorker," Charles promised. "She won't be any trouble at all."

Amy tugged on her mother's sleeve. "Let us have Rascal, Mama!"

Louisa offered Sallie a wry smile. "Looks like your brood has done decided this one for ya."

"Children," said Sallie, "you can have Rascal only if you're on perfect behavior until we leave Detroit."

"We'll be good, Mama!" came a chorus of promises.

"Then we accept your gift, Mr. Quigley."

"I'll see to it the dog is on the boat, in her own crate, just before departure," Quigley said. "Good evening, folks. Rascal, come!"

The dog followed obediently.

Sarah chattered excitedly about Rascal, but Jacob found his thoughts on the dog's owner. Quigley seemed likable, leaving Jacob to wonder why bad feelings flowed between him and Will. Perhaps someday he'd learn the story.

When he arrived back at the hotel room with Louisa, Elizabeth, and the Knight brood, he marveled that somehow, everyone managed to find a place to sprawl out for the night. He worried that Elizabeth wouldn't get much sleep, crammed into a bed with two other women. Sandwiched in on his small patch of floor between Will and the stack of Indian wares, he realized a long night lay ahead.

When morning came, Jacob was the first one up, stiff and sore. A cool breeze had come up, fluttering the curtains. He stepped over sleeping children to close the window, and was about to go back to bed when Will arose, groaning and moaning.

"Jacob, rub my shoulders," Will half-whispered, his head cocked off to one side. "I've got to get this kink out of my neck, and get on down to the capitol to file papers for the bank. I want to find more prospects for my land, too. I need to sell more parcels before Louisa and I go to New York."

Evidently awakened by Will's voice, Louisa whispered, "Aren't ya gonna eat breakfast first, Will?"

"No. You go with the others. I'll be back to take the midday meal with you."

As Jacob worked his fingers around the knotted muscle

in his uncle's neck, he asked, "Have you any suggestions where Elizabeth and I will find the best barter for Beloved-of-the-Forest and Walks Tall?"

"Jefferson Avenue is the place to go," Will said, slowly straightening his head. "Nearly every house between Shelby and Randolph Streets has been fitted up as a store and filled with goods. Ned Griswold, at Griswold's Dry Goods, was giving three iron pans for a deer hide awhile back." He moved his head from side to side, grimacing. "That'll have to do, Jacob. I've got to be on my way. You be sure and tell Ned I sent you. I bought over a hundred dollars' worth of goods from him last time I was in his place. If you don't like his first offer, you remind him of that."

"Thanks, Uncle Will. I appreciate the suggestion."

Later, Jacob took Elizabeth with him to the store Will had described. The place was abuzz with shoppers, and the bells on the door were constantly jingling with their comings and goings. While Jacob waited his turn behind several others to show the shopkeeper their Indian goods, Elizabeth browsed for the items Beloved-of-the-Forest wanted in trade.

On a shelf was a woolen blanket that could replace the Indian woman's worn-out one. Beloved-of-the-Forest would use it for a winter coat. She had already converted her old one into a strainer for maple sap, linings for moccasins, and a coat for one of the Indian children, so it was a necessity to find a new one before the cold season arrived.

Elizabeth made a mental note about the blanket, and continued browsing among the piece goods, trims, and iron pots.

Eager for Jacob to work a deal, she joined him at the

counter where he was now next in line. Jars of delicious-looking candy sticks lined the shelf, and she was tempted to indulge, but she resisted the urge.

When the tall, lean shopkeeper finished wrapping the previous order and putting the payment in his cash box, he focused on Jacob.

"What can I do for you, sir?"

"Are you Mr. Griswold?" Jacob asked.

"Yes, sir. How can I help you?"

"My uncle, Will Morgan, sent me here."

The bells on the door jingled again, diverting Mr. Griswold's attention to the customer entering the store—a tall young man of about twenty-five whose dark, wavy hair fell down to brush against his forehead.

"Governor Mason! Come for your sassafras sticks, have you?" Griswold asked with a grin.

"You know me too well, Mr. Griswold," the Governor said, approaching the counter.

"Was that ten sticks of sassafras you wanted, Governor?" He lifted the glass top from the jar.

"Yes, but wait on this couple here, first."

"I think you'd better go ahead, Governor," Jacob told him. "My transaction isn't nearly so simple as yours. But if I could impose a little, I'd be highly honored to shake your hand. I'm Jacob Morgan, and this is my wife, Elizabeth."

The young politician shook heartily. "Morgan of Riverton?" he asked.

Jacob nodded.

"Then you must be related to Will Morgan."

"Yes, sir. He's my uncle. Do you know him?"

"We've had many a lengthy discussion about his plans

for Riverton, Will and I. The last time we spoke, he was thinking of starting a bank. How is he, anyway?"

"Uncle Will is fine. In fact, he got married just a few days ago."

"I never would have expected that!" said the Governor.

"It's true. He's brought his new wife to Detroit for their wedding trip. In a few days, they're going on to New York City. He's filing articles here for incorporation of his bank, then he's going East to get the bank notes printed."

"Then congratulations are in order for both his marriage, and his bank! But I'd like to extend them in person. Can the four of you come to dinner at my house this evening?"

Jacob turned to Elizabeth.

"We'd be glad to come to dinner," she quickly replied, hoping Sallie and Isaac would understand.

"I'll see you about six, then," the Governor said. "Where are you staying, anyway? The hotels and rooming houses are full up."

"We're at the Woodworth Hotel," Jacob answered. "It was mighty cozy last night, with ten of us in the same room. Elizabeth's relatives are in the process of moving to Riverton from York State, and they had nowhere else to stay until the steamer takes us all up North."

The Governor shook his head. "No sense in crowding in like that when I have a houseful of empty rooms. Starting tonight, all ten of you will stay with me."

"We couldn't possibly impose on you like that," Jacob said.

Elizabeth nudged him hard, eager to be free of the cramped hotel room, but Jacob continued. "The Knights have four children. It would be too much."

"I'd be delighted to hear the voices of children in my house," Governor Mason insisted. "Move your things as soon as you finish with Mr. Griswold. I'll send a message to my hired woman to expect you."

"Thank you, Governor," Elizabeth said, hoping this wasn't a dream.

"We have only one problem," said Jacob. "We've got a large quantity of Indian goods stored in our room. We're hoping to work a deal with Mr. Griswold in barter for some things the Chippewas really need."

"We have superb birch bark baskets, moccasins, and hides," Elizabeth said, showing the wares.

Griswold inspected them, nodding agreement. "These are high quality goods. There's plenty of folks who'll want them."

"Good!" said Governor Mason. Turning to Jacob and Elizabeth, he said, "You and your relatives move to my place this afternoon, and we'll all sit down to dinner together this evening." He reached in his pocket for a coin and set it on the counter. "I'll take those sassafras sticks now, Mr. Griswold, and you'd better make it twenty, with children coming to my house."

CHAPTER

12

When the wagon carrying the Knights, the Morgans, and their belongings pulled up in front of Governor Mason's home at 303 Jefferson Avenue, Elizabeth was surprised at the modest nature of the house. The two-story brick structure was not particularly large or distinctive, with seven steps leading to an arched doorway, two windows on the first floor, and three identical ones in a row on the second floor. Within minutes, the Knights had been shown to a suite of garden-level rooms, Louisa and Will to an upstairs bedroom, and Elizabeth and Jacob to one across the hall.

Despite the home's nondescript exterior, Elizabeth found her bedroom—one normally occupied by the Governor's parents when they were in town—very inviting. The mahogany bedstead had maple rails overdraped with white mull curtains, and thick down-filled ticking on a hair mattress. To one side was a corner basin stand with gilt brass lion-mask knobs, and on the opposite side stood a tilt-top candle stand.

A set of steps much akin to those found in libraries drew her attention. The unequal heights of the risers seemed a bit odd until Elizabeth realized that the second tread lifted up, and its riser slid forward, creating a commode.

"Look, Jacob!" she said, delighted with her discovery. "We'll have to put one of these in our new house."

Jacob closed the drawer of the mahogany wardrobe where he was storing his belongings to inspect the piece, running his hand over its smooth, dark finish. "This is lovely—mahogany over tulip poplar and pine. And the covering on the treads looks like Brussels carpet. Very expensive." Giving Elizabeth's hand a squeeze, he said, "If you'll make needlepoint treads, I'll see to it you have a set of bed steps just like these for your new home."

She kissed his cheek. "Thank you, my darling. They'll look so much more handsome than a chamber pot. Then all we'll need is a bed like this one to step up into."

"Now *that* would take some doing. I can't promise you one this fancy, but we'll have something substantially better than the cot in the cabin."

The tall clock interrupted their conversation with its hour song, surprising Elizabeth with six chimes. "Is it really so late?"

Jacob consulted his watch, and nodded. "We're supposed to be downstairs for dinner now."

As Elizabeth descended to the first floor, she could hear the voices of Will, Louisa, and Governor Mason in the hallway. The Knights arrived at the same time as Jacob and Elizabeth.

The Governor gestured toward the dining room. "The cook tells me dinner is ready. Mrs. Morgan," he referred to Louisa, "would you be my hostess for this evening?" He offered her his arm.

"Well, think of that! Louisa exclaimed, "hostess at the Governor's dinner table!"

"Now don't go getting all swelled-headed over it," Will

warned, following behind the odd couple. "You know when we get back to Riverton, you'll be serving me up at that scarred old deal table in your cabin."

"Maybe so, but this here's a mem'ry to pass on to my grandchildren." When she stepped into the dining room, she paused, a look of astonishment on her face. "Land sakes! I've never seen so much silver as what's on that table. Why, there's at least two of everything. And them dishes—real porcelain." She held a saucer to the light from the window. "I can pretty nearly see right through it! This ain't nothin' like my tin plates up north."

Governor Mason laughed. "Your tin plates will probably outlast this Wedgewood."

"This really is too lovely," said Sallie. "The children should eat in the kitchen. I'd be horrified if they broke anything. They're accustomed to stoneware."

"No one but the cook eats in my kitchen," the Governor insisted. "All day, I've been looking forward to having children at my table."

When everyone had been seated, Louisa said, "Governor, would ya ask a blessin'?"

Head bowed, he said, "Lord, bless this food to our use, and these guests to your service as we strive together to bring honor and glory to you and to the State of Michigan. Amen."

"Amen." The word echoed around the table.

As the cook served herb soup in Wedgewood bowls, and Governor Mason inquired of the Knight children about their trip from York State, Elizabeth admired her surroundings. A Hepplewhite sideboard stood against the wall, its mahogany finish matching that of the table, while the bamboo-style chairs stood in stark contrast, having been painted the shade of rich cream and trimmed with dark green. The china pattern, lag-and-feather in sepia and gold, matched the ivory walls and green draperies, and complemented the feathery design on the handles of the silver.

When the soup course had been cleared away and crown roast of beef with parsley potatoes served all around, conversation turned to recent visitors at the Governor's home.

"Last summer, I had the privilege of entertaining Harriet Martineau when she passed through Detroit," said the Governor.

"She caused quite a stir back East with her support for the Abolitionist Party last year," said Isaac. "It was all over the papers in Rochester."

The Governor nodded. "I'm afraid it put her in disfavor with some folks, but it didn't seem to spoil her sojourn in Michigan. After she left Detroit, she wrote to say she and her fellow travelers stayed with a Michigan man who had bought eighty acres at a dollar apiece four years ago. Last year, he turned down twenty dollars an acre for the same land. It seems he'd shot a hundred deer in his woods and had sold them for three dollars each!"

"Did you hear that, Isaac and Jacob?" asked Will. "There's no telling how much Riverton property will be worth a few years from now!"

"I can't get over the number of people coming West," said Sallie. "From what I've seen since we arrived, Detroit is bursting at the seams."

"It's not quite as overcrowded as it was in the spring of last year," said Governor Mason. "On the twenty-third of May, seven hundred passengers disembarked here, and on average, a wagon left the city for the interior once every five minutes during the twelve hours of daylight."

"Charles, can you cipher how many wagons left on that day?" Isaac asked.

Charles thought a moment. "One hundred and forty-four."

"Very good, Charles!" said Elizabeth. "You must have been a star pupil in school."

"He was the smartest one in class!" Todd boasted.

Charles's cheeks flushed, and sensing his embarrassment, Elizabeth turned to a different topic. "Governor, isn't there a new steamboat named after you?"

Louisa spoke up. "Yeah, Governor. Is it true, what we overheard in the hotel? That there's a boat named the *Governor Mason?*"

The Governor nodded and smiled. "On the fourteenth of June, the village of Grand Rapids launched a boat by that name." He gave a description of the vessel, and other visitors to Michigan in recent weeks. When the table had been cleared and he saw that the cook was ready to bring out the dessert, he said, "Knowing that we would have a newlywed couple at the table, I asked the cook to prepare a special treat in honor of Will and Louisa."

When the cook entered carrying a three-layer cake piled high with white frosting, Louisa exclaimed, "Well bust my corset laces! Ya mean I'm actually gonna get to eat a piece of weddin' cake, after all?"

Elizabeth joined Will and Jacob in hearty laughter that left puzzled looks on the faces of the Knights and the Governor.

When the laughter had quieted, Louisa said, "Gov'nor Mason, I sure do thank ya for this cake. One of the ladies at Riverton baked us one almost as fine as this. Only trouble was, a big old bear invited himself to the party and ruined it before anyone got a taste!"

Governor Mason chuckled. "Cook, cut generous pieces all around!"

"Yes, sir," said the elderly woman, taking the silver cake server in hand.

When the meal had ended, Jacob retired to the drawing room with the other men, and discussion soon turned to Will's upcoming trip to New York City.

"I'll be going East soon, too," said Governor Mason. "The legislature has given approval to obtain a substantial loan for internal improvements. Roads and railroads are planned. And a significant amount of canal work is to be done on the rivers—the Kalamazoo, the Grand, the Sault St. Marie—and the Saginaw."

"Jacob, Isaac, I hope you're listening," said Will excitedly. "Our land's guaranteed to increase in value with the improvements the Governor wants to make."

"Governor, I'm surprised you've been able to find funding," Isaac observed. "The East is still hard-pressed over the banking panic."

"There's no doubt loans are difficult to come by," the Governor admitted, "but I've found some financiers who are very interested in investing in Michigan's future. I expect all the development plans to be approved by the legislature come spring. Then we can hire men to get started on these projects."

The conversation continued for some time on the future of Michigan until Isaac excused himself to retire. The pause in the discussion provided Jacob an opening to approach other questions that were on his mind.

"Governor, I know how committed you are to improving conditions in the rural areas of Michigan. I have an idea—albeit a small one—where you can help along those lines. It concerns Uncle Will's trip to New York."

When Jacob had made his suggestion, the Governor said, "Thank you for your recommendation. I'll see that I do my part before Will goes East."

"I'm much obliged, Governor. Now, if I may change the subject for a moment, I'm wondering if you know of any cabinetmakers in Detroit who might be willing to take on some work for me? My wife has been admiring the furnishings in our room, and I've promised to see what I can do to obtain similar pieces."

"One cabinetmaker comes immediately to mind," the Governor replied. "He's as good as the man who made our pieces in New York City, but a lot closer. George Quigley, over on Larned Street."

"George Quigley!" Will spat out the name like a curse. "Surely you can't mean to recommend that scoundrel."

The Governor's expression was one of complete bewilderment. "Are we talking about the same man? The George Quigley I'm speaking of is a large, heavy-set fellow with a rough-looking face."

"He's the one," Will replied, "but you don't know him like I do. Jacob, you stay clear of him!" Will punched the air with his finger. "He's a dangerous, unpredictable type."

"Now you've got me curious," said the Governor. "What dealings did you have with Mr. Quigley that earned him a reputation as such a despicable character?"

A silent moment passed before Will answered. "My acquaintance with Quigley goes back a few years, to when I first came to Michigan. I can tell you firsthand, he has little regard for the law. Many's the day I wished I'd never

155

crossed his path."

"But he saved Sarah Knight's life!" Jacob countered. "She would have surely been run over by a freight wagon last night, if not for Quigley."

Lines of skepticism marred Will's forehead. "Louisa told me all about what happened in front of the hotel. And the Knight children have been full of talk about the spaniel puppy Quigley promised them, but I'm not fooled by any of it," Will claimed. "That man has a dark side he hasn't revealed to either of you, and if you're wise, Jacob, you'll find someone else to do your work. In fact, I'd be more than happy to help you."

"It's not quite that simple, Uncle Will. You'll be gone a whole month, and I can't afford to hold up progress that long. You know I'm trying to finish the house as much as possible before winter sets in."

Will nodded thoughtfully. "All I can say is, if you must hire someone, don't hire Quigley."

Jacob went with his uncle each of the next three days to see about selling land to the emigrants arriving in Detroit. He sold two of the eight lots his uncle had given him, earning enough to pay off the debt he'd incurred for lumber at the Upper Saginaw mill, and for the taxes that would be due on his land. He was equally pleased when Will found a buyer by the name of Vickers for his own holdings. He paid enough in cash to cover Will's trip to New York with some left over. As an added bonus, Mr. Vickers was willing to become a part of the bank, so his name was substituted for Jacob's as one of the twelve directors.

On the last day before the *Governor Marcy* was scheduled to head north, Jacob and Elizabeth saw Will and

Louisa off on the *Ohio*, then Jacob went on his own to seek out Quigley's workshop on Larned Street. Will and the Governor's conflicting opinions about the cabinetmaker, and Jacob's own experiences with him, had become a troubling conundrum. Jacob had prayed about his need of furniture, and felt compelled to investigate Quigley further.

The front display windows of Quigley's Fine Furniture showed a chest and tall clock in an Empire design. The pieces were fashioned of mahogany, finished to a fine patina. The drawers were skillfully put together with dovetail joints.

As Jacob stepped through the open front door of the shop, the fragrance of fresh wood provided a welcome change from the odors of the well-traveled street on this hot afternoon. Quigley was unaware of his presence, bent over a table leg held in the vice attached to his workbench. He sanded with great concentration while whistling the tune to *Amazing Grace*. Jacob waited until he had finished the verse before announcing his presence.

"Good afternoon, Mr. Quigley."

The large gentleman looked up, seemingly pleased to see him. "Good afternoon, Mr. Morgan!"

Rascal came bounding out of the back room, her whole body wagging with her tail as she danced about the wood shavings at Jacob's feet. He stooped to pet her.

"Come for the dog, have ya? I understood the *Governor Marcy* was to be leavin' on the morrow. Captain Winthrop wouldna changed his plan, now, would he?" Quigley set down his sandpaper, pulled out the handkerchief hanging from his back pocket, and mopped away the perspiration that had begun to trickle down the side of his face.

"I'm not here about the dog, Mr. Quigley. I came to see about some furniture I need for the house I'm building in Riverton. Governor Mason referred me to you."

"The Governor, eh? I've done a fair amount of work for him and his kin. What did ya have in mind?"

"I'm in need of several pieces, but first, we'd better address the subject of payment. With money scarce, I'm wondering if you're amenable to taking some Riverton lots in trade for your labor?"

At the unexpected offer, Quigley's eyes narrowed to slits. With an obvious effort to keep his enthusiasm in check, he casually asked, "Did I hear you right? You have Riverton lots to barter?"

"Yes, sir. They front on the Saginaw River. They were deeded over to me by my Uncle Will. The other night, you said you knew his holdings well, so I assume you're familiar with the property."

Quigley reflectively scratched the stubble on his cheek. "I know the land. Is it still in forest?"

"Yes, sir. Mostly pine. It would serve well beneath the veneers of finer woods."

"I wasn't thinking so much about makin' furniture out of it, as I was of buildin' a cabin."

"There's plenty of timber for that," Jacob assured him, "but judging from your advice to Mr. Knight, I thought you were loyal to Detroit."

Quigley offered a wry smile. "I just didn't want your uncle takin' unfair advantage of Mr. Knight. Bargains on land are common in this town—especially with the shortage of cash money. As for the trade you suggest, I'm interested, but I'm wonderin' what your uncle has to say about it?"

"I didn't discuss it with him. I make my own decisions,

Mr. Quigley. If you agree to the trade I've suggested, I'll tell my uncle about it when he and his bride return from York State next month."

"Will Morgan is married?" Quigley's voice held surprise.

"Yes, sir, to a woman who was widowed up in Riverton. They've gone to get bank notes engraved for the Saginaw Valley Bank my uncle has chartered."

Quigley ran his hand over the table leg he'd been sanding. He whistled softly while he glanced about the shop as if taking inventory.

Jacob regonized the tune, *God Moves in a Mysterious Way*, and felt reassured that Quigley couldn't possibly be the nasty man Will had described. He was praying that God's will be done regarding the deal he had proposed, when Quigley spoke again.

"Mr. Morgan, if you and I are gonna do business together, we'd best get down to details. Just exactly how much furniture did ya want, and how much land did ya have to offer?"

Jacob pulled some papers from his pocket. "It's all in writing—my list of needs, and the deeds to my Riverton property."

Through the course of discussion, Quigley suggested that some of the work Jacob was seeking could be best accomplished on site. Jacob wrote up an agreement which they both signed. When the chimes of the tall clock rang, Jacob was surprised that two hours had passed.

Quigley saw him to the door, offering his hand. "I'll be up to start work in your house in about a fortnight, Mr. Morgan—the next time the *Governor Marcy* goes North. Meanwhile, I'll finish the pieces I've promised my other customers, put my shop in order, and prepare to close down for a time. I'm looking forward to living up North for a spell."

"I'll make sure at least one room in the new house is habitable before you arrive," Jacob assured him. "Good day!"

CHAPTER

13

The day Jacob returned to Riverton, he and the other town's residents helped Isaac Knight temporarily settle his family into the quarters Will had occupied on the upper level of his blockhouse. The next morning, Isaac and several others made a start on his smithy. The plan included modest living quarters in the rear. Sallie was too eager for a place of their own to wait until their cabin could be erected on the lot north of Jacob's house.

While efforts got underway on the smithy, Jacob took Elizabeth to the Chippewa village. When Beloved-of-the-Forest and Walks Tall learned the extent of the goods waiting for them in Will's blockhouse, they promised to come the next day with two canoes to fetch their supplies.

The following morning, Brother-of-the-Wolf came with the Chippewa couple in a separate canoe. His face had healed well since his confrontation with the bear, and according to the Clarkes, his esteem in the Saginaw Valley had reached almost legendary proportions since his triumphant kill at the wedding feast.

While Elizabeth was showing Beloved-of-the-Forest about the domestic items she had earned in trade for her baskets and moccasins, Jacob presented Walks Tall with the rifle and knife his animal hides had brought. When the goods had been packed in the bottom of the birch bark vessels, Brother-of-the-Wolf approached Jacob.

"Brother-of-the-Wolf owns many hides. You trade for gun and knife?" He indicated Walks Tall's weapons.

Jacob sensed an underlying competitiveness in Brother-of-the-Wolf. Now that Walks Tall owned the finest hunting weapons of anyone in the Chippewa village, Brother-of-the-Wolf wanted their equal. His request provided an opening for a barter of a different kind.

"I will trade for Brother-of-the-Wolf," Jacob answered, "if Brother-of-the-Wolf will teach me how he hunts."

Silent moments passed before the Indian gave a solemn nod. "Brother-of-the-Wolf teach Jacob to hunt . . . *after* Jacob make trade."

Jacob offered his hand. "Agreed."

Brother-of-the-Wolf grasped it firmly. "Agreed."

One afternoon a week later, when Jacob was struggling to finish the wainscoting in the dining room of his new house, he heard the unmistakable sound of the *Governor Marcy's* whistle. Captain Winthrop must have loaded his cargo deck more quickly than usual in Detroit. He set his hammer and nails aside and hurried to the blockhouse to get out the hides Brother-of-the-Wolf had brought for trade. As the boat approached the dock, Jacob was surprised and pleased to see a passenger he recognized waving to him from the deck.

"Hello, Mr. Morgan!"

"Welcome to Riverton, Mr. Quigley!" Jacob shouted above the noise of the engine. "I wasn't expecting you for another week."

"Guess Cap'n Winthrop was plum eager to get away from the heat of the city," Quigley hollered back.

When the boat was made fast, Jacob negotiated a deal with Captain Winthrop for freight and barter on Brother-of-the-Wolf's behalf. When the terms were agreed, he again turned his attention to Quigley. "I'm glad you're here. It's been a struggle for me, working alone inside the house this past week. I haven't made much progress."

"Soon as I get my wood unloaded, I want you to show me your place," said Quigley.

Jacob helped the older man carry most of his mahogany boards into the blockhouse. Balancing the last load on his shoulder, he headed up the riverbank. "This way to my new house, Mr. Quigley."

Quigley slung his pack over his shoulder and followed Jacob up the log stairs. At the top of the riverbank, Isaac Knight, his two sons, and several other men were busy putting up a smithy. Quigley made mention of the fact that several log cabins were visible where only one had stood in years past.

Jacob led Quigley south on a well-traveled trail, catching a glimpse of his frame house through the pines. In the distance, he heard a familiar bark, and soon Quigley was being besieged by Rascal. The two Knight girls and their mother followed close behind. After a pleasant exchange, Sarah and Amy ran off down the path, Rascal nipping at their heels.

As Jacob continued on his way, his stomach growled, and he checked his watch. "It's getting late, Mr. Quigley. After I show you the house, I'll take you to the cabin and Elizabeth will feed us supper. You're probably hungry after traveling all day."

Quigley patted his oversized stomach. "I've never been known to pass up a homecooked meal."

When the cabinetmaker had finished going over the work to be done at the house, he followed Jacob into the settlement east of the river.

"Elizabeth and I are temporarily living in Mr. LaMore's cabin," Jacob explained. "He's away in Canada, but he's coming back sometime next month, so I'm eager to finish the house as soon as possible." He pointed down the trail. "There's our cabin. At the very edge of the forest."

Quigley's expression became pensive, then tight with some other, harsher emotion. He read the sign on the door out loud. "'Jacob Morgan, Elizabeth Morgan—Medicine Lady.' Pretty fancy, that."

"Uncle Will made it for us soon after we arrived," Jacob explained. "Elizabeth's father is a doctor out East, and she picked up a good bit of knowledge, helping him in his practice."

Jacob opened the door. Elizabeth was standing at the hearth, and she greeted them with a smile. "Mr. Quigley, you took me by surprise. I wasn't expecting you till next week. But I've got plenty of stew to go around tonight. You *do* like squirrel stew, don't you?"

"Yes, ma'am," Quigley replied absently. He seemed to take in every corner of the single room, every detail, as if each had personal meaning to him.

"Make yourself at home, Mr. Quigley," said Jacob, taking his pack and stowing it in the corner.

The words appeared to draw Quigley from reminiscences. "I'd better wash for supper," he told Jacob.

"Come on. I'll take you to the village well," he offered, picking up a bucket, towel, and a piece of soap on his way out the door.

Several minutes later, when Elizabeth had set a pot of

164

stew and a plate of hot biscuits on the table, Jacob said, "Mr. Quigley, would you like to ask a blessing?"

The request apparently pleased the older man. He bowed his head and folded his hands. "Dear Lord, Thank ya for this food. Thank ya for the good company of Mr. and Mrs. Morgan, and give us y'r blessin's. In the name of the Father, the Son, and the Holy Ghost, Amen."

"Amen," replied Jacob and Elizabeth.

She passed the plate of biscuits and pot of stew. "Help yourself, Mr. Quigley. Eat hearty. You've got a lot of hard work ahead of you in the days to come, and leftovers don't keep."

"I'll take you at your word, Mrs. Morgan." He put four biscuits on his plate, split them open, and drowned them with stew. "Mrs. Morgan, this is the Chippewa way of cookin' squirrel, isn't it? It's excellent!"

"Thank you, Mr. Quigley. How did you know?"

"My wife used to make it this way. I always loved White Dove's cookin', but her squirrel stew was particularly fine." He tasted another mouthful.

"Mr. Quigley, you said you knew this area well. Was White Dove from the Chippewa village just north of here?" Jacob asked.

Quigley nodded and swallowed heavily. "In the years before this land went up for sale, I settled here among the Chippewas to trap and hunt. After a time, I took White Dove for my wife." He set down his fork and wiped his mouth. "Fact is, we lived right here, in this very cabin."

Jacob read the curious look on Elizabeth's face and spoke again. "You must have been here when Uncle Will bought this section in '34. I'm surprised you didn't buy it for yourself."

Quigley tucked into the stew again, but his appetite seemed to wane with talk of land sales. "I had a mind to buy this section. I went down to Detroit to make the claim, but things just didn't work out." Abruptly, he changed the subject. "Now, tell me somethin', Mr. and Mrs. Morgan. Do you believe in miracles?"

"I do," said Jacob.

"Miracles are in the Bible, and I believe God's word," Elizabeth reasoned.

"Good. 'Cause you're lookin' at a miracle," Quigley stated. After a moment's pause, he laughed. "I might be the sorriest lookin' miracle you ever laid eyes on, but the fact I'm alive is the *real* miracle. Ya see, I nearly died of cholera in the summer of '34. It struck Detroit in the first week of August. In twenty days, a hundred and twenty-two people died."

"I remember now, Uncle Will mentioned the epidemic in a letter," said Jacob, spearing a morsel of squirrel meat. "He said seven percent of the city's population was killed by the disease."

"That's right," said Quigley. "They used to toll the bell for every death, but when the cholera got bad, the ringing just made people panic, so Mayor Trowbridge put a stop to it."

"There couldn't possibly have been enough doctors to go around," said Elizabeth, sprinkling a touch more salt on her stew.

"You're right, Mrs. Morgan," said Quigley. "The doctors worked day and night. But there was some patients they plum gave up on. Then the volunteers took over.

"Father Kundig bought an old Presbyterian Church and set up a hospital. Then he fitted up a one-horse ambulance and made the rounds of the city, mornin' and night." Quigley paused for a heaping forkful of stew, downing it with a long draft of cold well water.

Elizabeth spoke during his silence. "Didn't the priest get sick, himself?"

Quigley swallowed the last of his water and set down his empty cup. "People went out of their way to avoid him, figurin' he was contagious, but he never did come down with the cholera."

"That sounds like a miracle, too," Jacob observed.

The comment made Quigley smile. "I believe you're right. That makes this the story of *two* miracles!"

"The epidemic must have been awfully hard on the families it touched," said Elizabeth, rising to refill Quigley's cup from the bucket by the hearth. "There must have been families without mamas, families without papas, and couples left without children."

Quigley nodded. "There were. But the worst was when both the parents died. Some of 'em even knew beforehand the cholera was gonna make orphans of their little ones, and they gave them to Father Kundig to look after."

"A priest with children," Jacob concluded. "Sounds like they needed an orphanage."

"They did. And the good ladies of Father Kundig's parish helped him to establish one. But that was after the epidemic was over. I haven't finished tellin' ya what happened when the disease was at its worst.

"I told ya how Father Kundig rigged up an ambulance. Well, he used come past my shop twice every day. In the mornin', I'd wave to him from the front door. At night, I'd be out on the street, burnin' pitch. The air was real heavy, and that was supposed to purify it. So a couple of fellas on

167

each block would see to the task. I'd be out, tendin' my kettle by the time the good Father came by for his second round of the day."

"The city must have smelled awful, with all that black smoke in the air," said Elizabeth, wrinkling her nose.

"To this day, the smell of pitch puts a real sick feeling inside me," said Quigley, taking a swallow of water before he continued. "Worst part is, it didn't keep the cholera away. After awhile, I took sick. When Father Kundig saw that I wasn't at my work, he came into my shop. There I was, burnin' up with fever on the bed in my back room.

"He put me on his wagon and took me to his hospital. That night, he said the rosary over me. I told him his prayers were a waste. I said I hadn't believed in God for a real long time. I'd known Christians who did real bad things. Some of 'em were right in my own family!

"But Father Kundig wouldn't give up on me. Every night, he came back to my bedside and prayed the rosary. I got so sick, after awhile I didn't even know he was there.

"Then, the fever let up and I started feelin' better. Father Kundig read the Bible to me. He reminded me how Jesus died on the cross to save me. I'd put that out of my mind many years before. I wasn't ready to think about it again. But a verse Father Kundig read from the Bible stuck in my mind. I'd learned it as a small boy. 'For God so loved the world—'"

Elizabeth and Jacob joined him on the rest of the verse, "—that he gave his only begotten Son, that whosoever believeth in him should not perish, but have everlasting life.'"

"John, Chapter Three, verse sixteen," said Jacob, reaching for another biscuit. "That's the first Bible verse I ever learned."

"Me, too," said Elizabeth, passing the pot of stew to Jacob.

"It really set me to thinkin'," said Quigley. "There was a family with six children. The youngest one died in Father Kundig's hospital, and his parents were deep in grief. They never would have given up that boy willingly. The fact that they had five other little ones didn't seem to be much consolation.

"So the verse in John kept comin' back to me. God had only one son, yet he gave up that son by choice, to save us. I couldn't reckon how painful that must have been."

"So the miracle happened. You found God again," Elizabeth surmised.

Quigley smiled. "Not quite yet. I'm a stubborn man. I clung to my old hurts. But when the epidemic was over, Father Kundig came by my shop and invited me to his church services. I didn't want to go, but I couldn't turn him down. I'd have died if he hadn't taken care of me, and we both knew it. So I went to his church. Week after week, I sat in the pew and learned about God. And after a fashion, I came to know God again. And *that's* the miracle of George Quigley. God took an angry, unbelieving, sick man, made him well again, and saved him by grace."

"Amen!" said Jacob.

"Amen!" Elizabeth echoed.

"Of course, I'm by no means a perfect man," Quigley hastily claimed. "I still have a temper. Especially when I see someone takin' unfair advantage. That gets my dander up quicker than anything else. But I've learned how to forgive. And the resentment that ruled me for so long has been cleansed from my heart. It leaves me in a spirit to appreciate the good things in life, like this here stew of yours, Mrs. Morgan. It's good to the last bite." He popped his last piece into his mouth.

"Could I interest you in a bowl of apple pudding for dessert?" Elizabeth asked.

"If your puddin' is anywhere near as tasty as your stew, I'd be a fool to turn it down," Quigley said.

"Maybe over dessert, you could tell us more about White Dove," Elizabeth suggested. "You only said you married her, nothing more—or am I prying?"

"I can satisfy your curiosity about White Dove real quick. She died givin' birth to our first child two years after we married. The baby died with her. Now I've done enough talkin' for one night. I'd like to hear about you folks, for a change."

Elizabeth dished up the dessert while Jacob told of their courtship and wedding. When he came to the part about their arrival in Riverton, she contributed some words of her own.

"I was so angry to discover Uncle Will's map was nothing like the real town of Riverton, I would have left the same day I came, if he hadn't stopped me!"

"You mean he didn't even tell *you*, his own kin, that this was mostly forest?" Quigley asked.

"You must think I'm a real fool, not to have known," said Jacob, "but I'd never been here, or talked to anyone who had. Uncle Will's word was all I had to go on. And he has a way of making you believe what he says."

Quigley set his spoon in his empty dish. "You're no fool, Mr. Morgan. I can't tell you the number of land schemes I've heard about in Detroit. People by the hundreds have been taken in by them. It makes me angry to see it. That's why I said what I did when your uncle was talkin' to Mr. Knight in the tavern. I didn't want another emigrant gettin' a bad deal. I figured if he'd just take some time, he'd be able to bargain for a good price on land."

"My uncle settled on fair terms with Mr. Knight, after a fashion," said Jacob, "but I felt like I had to be there every minute to make sure he didn't overstate the conditions up here."

Quigley nodded, his expression thoughtful. Jacob studied the man he'd brought into his home and wondered what lay secreted behind that reminiscent look.

Three weeks later, Jacob stood back to admire the finish on the wainscoting in the dining room, then he took three deeds from his inside pocket and spread them out on the new table Quigley had made to his specifications. All of the cabinetmaker's work would be complete within a few more days, but Jacob couldn't wait any longer to show his appreciation for Quigley's expertise, and to officially make him his new neighbor.

He went to the back room to help Quigley clean brushes and put away supplies, as they had at the end of each day since they'd started working together.

"When we're done here, I want to show you something in the dining room," he told Quigley, slapping a brush against an old rag to dry the bristles.

"Uh, oh. I must've missed a spot when I was stainin'. Or did I put on the varnish coat too thick and get a run?"

Jacob chortled. "You know very well, the finish in there is perfect. My request isn't on the order of a complaint."

Quigley grinned. "Then I guess I'll have to honor it, won't I?" He gathered the brushes into a bouquet and dropped them into an old crock, hung the rags neatly over a line he'd strung across a corner, then followed Jacob into the dining room.

"These belong to you, now," said Jacob, indicating the deeds. "I've already signed them over to you."

"But my work isn't quite done, yet. I still have the—"

Jacob waved off the argument. "I wanted to give these to you now, to show you how much I appreciate the fine work you've put in. I'm sure you'll be finished with the job by the end of the week."

The conversation was interrupted by the sound of the front door opening, and Will's gravelly voice.

"Jacob?"

"In the dining room, Uncle Will."

He stepped through the door, freezing the moment he saw Quigley. "You lowdown, rotten . . . " His face grew scarlet with rage. "Get out!"

"Calm down, Uncle Will!" Jacob ordered.

Will ignored him, pulling a pistol from his inside pocket and aiming it at Quigley. "I said, get out, you scum!"

CHAPTER

14

Jacob planted himself in front of Will, pushing aside the weapon. "You've got no right to order this man out of my house."

Will shoved past Jacob, the barrel of his pistol inches from Quigley's chest. "You heard me. Get out!"

"Not until I've said my piece," Quigley replied. "I'm sorry for the hurt I caused ya back in '34."

Will cocked the hammer. "If you don't walk out the door by the time I count three, I'll have to carry you out. One . . . two . . ."

Quigley stood fast.

Jacob dove at Will. A shot went off as they fell to the floor. Jacob tried to wrestle the gun free.

Will rolled on top of him, pointing the barrel of the pistol at Jacob's neck. "Stay out of this, nephew, before you get hurt!"

Suddenly, Quigley's boot sent the pistol flying. He pulled Will off Jacob and threw him against the wall. "Don't do somethin' you'll regret!" he warned.

Will lunged at Quigley, taking him down. Jacob struggled to force his uncle off.

Will elbowed him in the gut and scrambled in the direction of his pistol.

Jacob got there first, kicking the weapon in Quigley's

direction.

The cabinetmaker picked up the gun and tossed it out an open window.

Will pulled himself up from the floor, his face scarlet with rage as he confronted Quigley. "I'm telling you to get out! And don't ever show your face in Riverton again!"

Quigley stood fast. "And *I'm* tellin' *you*, I'm *sorry* for what I did three years ago. I wanna make things right between us, if you'll just tell me how."

"What you took from me can't be replaced," Will said resentfully. "All I want from you now, is the sight of your backside, walking out of town."

Quigley stepped up to the dining table, gathered the deeds together, and handed them to Will. "I got no intention of leavin' Riverton, now that I own property here."

Jacob spoke up. "I bartered some of the lots you gave me in return for the work Mr. Quigley's doing in the house."

Will studied first one document, then another, then the last one, his head moving from side to side. Jogging the pages together, he ripped them to pieces and scattered them across the floor. "The deal's off, Quigley! Now, make yourself scarce!"

"He'll do no such thing!" Jacob countered. "You can tear up pieces of paper, but I won't let you renege on the deal you made with me!"

"I gave you those lots, I can take them back," Will claimed.

"It's too late for that," Quigley told Will. "Everybody hereabouts knows that land was passed from you to Jacob.

"The agreement was legal and binding," Jacob told his uncle. "Now, the property is Quigley's. You might as well get used to it."

"I'll never get used to it!" Will said bitterly. "That man burned up my cabin and everything that ever meant anything to me, all because I asked him to move off property that didn't belong to him."

Jacob flinched inwardly. "Mr. Quigley, is that true?

Quigley hung his head. "I'm ashamed to admit it. I acted out of pure anger." Facing Jacob, he continued. "Your uncle told me he wasn't filin' for this claim. He wanted a head start for the land office. He knew I'd take my time goin' to Detroit, since White Dove was heavy with child. When my wife and I got there, your uncle had already bought all the land hereabouts—including the section I was plannin' to buy and deed over to White Dove's people."

Jacob focused on Will. "Is Mr. Quigley telling the truth?"

Will drew a tight breath. "As far as it goes. He might have taken his time going south, but he didn't waste a minute coming back north and setting a torch to my place." He paused to swallow, and Jacob could see he was struggling with his emotions. "Jacob, do you remember Goldie, the dog I brought with me from Brockport?"

Jacob nodded. "She was the most beautiful retriever I've ever seen—real gentle, too."

"For five years, she was my best friend," Will said quietly. "Then Quigley set the fire, and . . . she died along with her six pups."

"I didn't know the dog was in there," Quigley claimed. "I never meant to hurt her."

Will cast him a venomous look. "You burned up my grandpa's journal about the war, too."

"Do you mean Great-grandfather Morgan's stories about General Knox?" Jacob wanted to know.

Will nodded.

"Papa told me a tale or two, but I've forgotten them now. I'd sure like to hear those stories again. I want to be able to tell them to my children."

Will's countenance turned reflective. He pulled out a dining chair. "Sit down, Jacob. You, too, Quigley. I'm going to tell you about Wilburforce Jacob Morgan, and one of his adventures, back when Knox was still a colonel." When the others were seated, Will continued. "Back in the winter of '76, the Americans had the British pinned in at Boston. General Washington wanted to attack, but his advisors said he shouldn't. So Colonel Knox came up with a plan. He said he'd take his artillery regiment up to Fort Ticonderoga and bring down the cannon and guns that had been captured from the British."

"That's a lot of miles," said Jacob.

"Nearly three hundred," said Will.

"I don't see how they coulda done it," Quigley observed.

"Colonel Knox was a big man," Will went on. "Bigger than even you, Quigley. Grandpa said he weighed over two hundred and fifty pounds, but he was full of energy. So he and his men used sleds and oxen to drag fifty-five pieces of artillery through the snow. Then General Washington put the guns up in Dorchester Heights. When General Howe saw them, he made a deal with Washington. Either the Americans could let him and his men leave the city peacefully, or they would destroy it. So Washington let them go, and the colonies were free of the British for a time."

"Your great-grandpappy did you proud, Jacob," Quigley said. "I'm mighty sorry his words got burned up in the fire, but you'll always have his story to tell."

"There was plenty more in that journal, too," Will said irritably. "Grandpa told how he went across the river at Trenton with Knox before Washington and the others made their crossing. And he told about the battles at Princeton and Germantown, and Monmouth and Yorktown. I've tried to write them down again, the best I remember them, but it's not the same as grandpa's telling of it."

Quigley shook his head remorsefully. "I really am sorry 'bout that journal."

"That's not the only one that burned," Will told him bluntly. "I kept diaries, too, from the time I was a boy. And every one of them went up in smoke."

"Oh, no," Jacob muttered sympathetically.

Will went on. "I wrote about the Erie being dug, and of my first days here in the wilderness. Now the diaries are gone."

"I can't get 'em back for ya, but like I said, I'll do just about anything to make it up to ya," Quigley offered again.

"Then give up the land!" Will demanded.

"Anything but that," Quigley answered with equal firmness.

Will rose so quickly, his chair nearly toppled over. "Stay, then. But keep out of my path." His boot heels clicked loudly on his way toward the door, then he abruptly turned to address Jacob. "I nearly forgot. Here's the reply you wanted from York State." He pulled an envelope from his inside pocket and tossed it in the direction of the table, then stomped out the door.

Jacob retrieved the missive from the floor, loosened the wax seal, and read eagerly, his heart filling with happiness.

"Listen to this!" he told Quigley, reading the letter aloud.

When he had finished, Quigley said, "I'm real happy for ya, Jacob."

Despite the cabinetmaker's words, Jacob sensed a rare melancholy about him. "Mr. Quigley, you're not worrying about the trouble with Uncle Will, are you?"

"It'd be a bold-faced lie to deny it. But I know in my heart what I gotta do. The Lord's put a real burden on me to stick around these parts. I can't up and leave, like y'r uncle wants."

"Then stay and do God's will. I'm proud to have you as my neighbor." He put his arm about Quigley's shoulder, earning an appreciative smile in return.

Elizabeth's throat had been sore all day long, and she knew it had nothing to do with the cold and wet late-October weather outside the cabin; rather, with the fact that she would soon be living hundreds of miles from Jacob. A few days ago, the *Governor Marcy* had come up the river bound for Upper Saginaw, and any day now, it would steam its way back downstream, headed for Detroit, with her aboard.

She had put off packing for as long as she could, and now the sad task was heavy upon her. As she filled her trunk with the baby quilt she had embroidered, the booties she had knit, the diapers and kimono Louisa had made months ago, and the tiny little moccasins Beloved-of-the-Forest had sewn, she tried not to think about the fact that Jacob wouldn't even see their child until it was at least two months old. *Dear Lord, help me to endure the separation until spring,* she silently prayed, *and bring me back safely so we can be a family.*

Inside her, the baby kicked. She placed her hand on her belly and felt it kick again. Bittersweet tears began to trickle down her cheeks. She was dabbing them away with her handkerchief when Jacob entered the cabin.

He caught a glimpse of the distraught look on his wife's face before she turned away, and knew she was trying to hide her sadness from him. He had been well aware of her melancholy since the *Governor Marcy* had come up past Riverton recently, and he asked himself again for the hundredth time whether he was doing the right thing, letting her prepare to leave Michigan. Crossing the crude puncheon floor and rag rug, he thought of the smooth pine boards in the new home he had just come from, the place where his first child would learn to crawl. He thought, too, of the man who had recently arrived in Riverton, unbeknownst to Elizabeth, and was helping to finish the work inside the new house days ahead of schedule. Thankfully, Elizabeth had obeyed Jacob's request to stay clear of the house for the past month, and was unaware of the exact situation there.

With the extra help Jacob had been given, the interior of both the first and second floors was now complete. He was so excited about it—and the special surprise he had in store for his wife—he could barely contain himself. But he kept a tight lid on his inner joy, and prevented any semblance of a smile from showing on his face.

Thoughts of his special gifts for Elizabeth were interrupted by her quiet sniffling, and he came beside her, taking her in his arms and turning her toward him. "My darling, don't be so sad. Think of the good time ahead. Soon, you'll be reunited with your father. Doesn't that make you happy?"

Elizabeth wiped her tears and gazed into Jacob's eyes. Forcing words past the lump in her throat, she replied in a shaky voice, "But *you* won't be there."

"I'll be with you in spirit," he said, kissing her forehead. "Now cheer up. I came home to tell you that Mr. Quigley went to Upper Saginaw this morning to buy paint, and he says that Captain Winthrop plans to depart for Detroit early tomorrow. Just think. Soon, you and the Clarkes will be on the *Governor Marcy*, and it won't be long till you're in Brockport again!"

Jacob's words only made Elizabeth more glum. She buried her face in his soft flannel shirt and sobbed.

He rubbed her back. "Don't cry, my precious. *Please* don't cry. You're breaking my heart. Now you've got to dry those tears and come with me to the new house. It's time for you to see how well it's coming. Besides, I'm desperate for your opinion on something."

She stifled her tears and blew her nose. "I'm in no mood to go to the new house, Jacob. It's too rainy right now. Besides, I look a fright, with my eyes all red and swollen. I hate for Mr. Quigley to see me looking this way."

Jacob kissed her briefly then leaned back, scrutinizing her appearance. "You look beautiful to me—more beautiful than the day we were married. As I recall, you shed some tears that day, too, but you weren't afraid for anyone to know you'd been crying."

Elizabeth almost smiled at Jacob's illogical comparison. "Tears of joy have a way of enhancing a woman's beauty. Tears of sorrow only elicit pity. Everyone in town knows I hate the thought of leaving you. I don't want them taking pity on me. Besides, I'm not nearly finished packing. If I don't get on with it, I won't be ready to get on the *Governor Marcy* tomorrow."

Jacob drew a deep breath. Puffing up his already broad chest, he took her firmly by the shoulders. "Elizabeth, I'm sorry, but I must insist you come with me to the house. I'll help you finish packing later. But right now, you've got to give approval for the blue paint Mr. Quigley mixed for the nursery." He fetched her mackintosh from its peg and held it for her.

Elizabeth knew better than to argue when Jacob got into his bossy moods. Adding a lightweight wool shawl to the cotton one already on her shoulders, she put on her raincoat and boots, pulled the hood up over her hair, and headed out the door, thankful for Jacob's arm about her that helped to thwart the wind whipping at the hems of her coat and skirt.

The cool, moist air was redolent with the scent of pine. Raindrops pelted her face and pattered against the rubberized cotton fabric of her coat. The trail to the house was full of puddles, and she dreaded the thought of tracking mud onto the new porch, but the soft ground couldn't be avoided, her feet sinking in a bit with each step.

The rain had let up by the time they reached the corner of Main Street and River Avenue. Smoke was rising from Isaac's new smithy. Sallie and the children were undoubtedly tucked into the small living quarters at the back, eager for the day their cabin would be ready. Elizabeth didn't envy them, all cramped in for the third day in a row of wet weather.

A minute later, when she came to the partially completed log walls on the Knights' lots adjacent to hers and Jacob's, Elizabeth wondered how long her aunt would have to wait for proper housing, with rain delaying construction frequently now that fall weather was here.

Jacob's gentle squeeze interrupted her thoughts. He pointed in the direction of their frame house. "We hung the shutters yesterday. Isaac made some mighty fancy hinges for them. They look nice, don't you think?"

Despite her somber mood, and the wet, miserable weather, Elizabeth smiled the moment she saw the house. The exterior appearance had changed appreciably since she'd last seen it, and she couldn't help but like her first glimpse of the freshly painted shutters and decorative wrought iron hinges.

"I can hardly believe it," she said, pausing to admire the effect. "The house looks just like I imagined it—just like you promised me it would—with those green shutters and the white clapboard siding. If it weren't for those bold, black hinges, our place would look identical to Papa's from the front."

"Didn't I promise you'd like it? Now, come along. You've got to see inside." He hustled her up the path that would some day be their front walk.

The moment he opened the door, the thick odor of fresh paint assaulted Elizabeth. She stepped onto an old sheet Jacob had used as a drop cloth over the entrance floor, thankful that the newly varnished maple would be somewhat protected from the mud on her boots and the moisture dripping from her coat.

"Let me help you with that," he said, unfastening her mackintosh before she could even push back the hood. He folded it and laid it on the cloth, then helped her take off her boots. As she waited for him to remove his own raincoat, she sensed something strange in the atmosphere that she had never noticed before—something other than the strong odor of paint and the shadowy darkness of the entryway. To her right, the dining room door was shut tight, and to her left, the parlor door stood closed. She concluded that the lack of light from those rooms made the front hall gloomier than usual. But when she started to open the parlor door, Jacob swiftly removed her hand from the knob.

"Uh, uh! You can't go in there just yet."

"But I only wanted to let in some light."

He smiled mischievously. "I'm hiding a special little something in there to show you later. But first, you must come into the kitchen. That's where I've been mixing up the paint. I've started a fire in the fireplace there to take off the chill." He led her by the hand down the hallway to the back of the house.

The door to the kitchen was closed, and Elizabeth noticed that Jacob paused before he grasped the knob. Swinging the door wide, he waited politely for her to pass through.

Stepping into the warmth and light, Elizabeth could not believe the sight that greeted her. There, beside the wide stone hearth, stood her papa, his full-bent pipe hanging from the corner of a smile wider than the Saginaw River.

"Elizabeth, my daughter, how I've missed you!" he said, coming toward her with outstretched arms.

She had just time enough to realize that the deep, mellow voice matched the vision before her when her consciousness started to fade away and she felt herself falling.

"Elizabeth!" Jacob cried, hurrying to catch her.

The sound of Jacob's panicky voice and the feeling of his strong arms cradling her, pushed back the gray veil that had started to obscure her world. He eased her down onto the floor, cradling her head on his knees. She blinked several times.

Her papa knelt beside her, gently slapping her cheeks. "Daughter, wake up! This is no time to go noodles on me. I haven't even unpacked my smelling salts yet!"

She offered a weak smile. "Sorry Papa. I guess the shock of seeing you here was a bit much." A rustling sound coming from the doorway drew her attention and she pushed herself up to see who was there.

Her Aunt Sallie stepped into the kitchen. "Elizabeth, are you all right?" The concern in her voice was reflected in the flush on her cheeks.

"Aunt Sallie, what are you doing here?"

Sallie pressed her lips together and stared at Jacob.

Elizabeth focused on her husband. "Jacob, will you please tell me what's going on?"

"Your aunt came to help me with the surprise in the front parlor," Jacob explained.

"As if the surprise in the kitchen wasn't enough!" Elizabeth said with a chuckle.

"Do you feel up to another surprise?" her father asked, stroking her forehead.

Elizabeth sat up straight. "Papa, you know me. I've always loved surprises. Just give me a sip of water, then I'll be ready to see what Jacob has hidden in the parlor."

While Sallie dipped water from a bucket near the hearth, a thought suddenly came to Elizabeth and she focused on her father. "Papa, I'm supposed to leave for Brockport tomorrow, but . . . "

He grinned widely. "No need. You can stay right here in Riverton to have your baby. Jacob's been kind enough to offer me accommodations in your new home for the winter. Next spring, I'll put up my own place."

Elizabeth's jaw dropped, and Jacob wrapped his arm tightly about her, fearing she might grow faint again.

Sallie offered Elizabeth a tin cup. "While you've got your mouth open, try putting some of this cold water in it. It's fresh from the well."

Elizabeth took several swallows, then dipped the corner of her apron in the water and patted her forehead and cheeks. Glancing from Jacob to her father and back again, she said, "I still can't get over it! Papa, here for the winter! I won't have to leave you, after all!"

Her eyes shined with unshed tears, and her happiness filled Jacob's heart with joy. He kissed her cheek. "I couldn't bear to have you leave. Nor could I stand the thought of spending the winter in this house alone."

"Now we can forget about those problems," Elizabeth said. Taking one more sip from the tin cup, she handed it back to Sallie. "Now what's this about a surprise in the front parlor?"

Hurriedly, Sallie put the cup away and headed for the door. "Just give me a few seconds to check on it one last time."

Her footsteps faded down the hallway as Jacob and Elizabeth's father helped her to her feet. Moments later, Sallie's voice echoed through the empty corridor. "You can bring Elizabeth in, now!"

Jacob's arm securely about her, she was headed for the kitchen door when she paused to face her father. "Papa, how did you get to Riverton from Detroit? You couldn't have come on the *Governor Marcy*, or I'd have known about it five days ago."

Her papa grinned. "Elizabeth, I'll explain everything to you after you've walked down that hall and opened the door to the parlor."

She started walking, then halted once again, turning to Jacob this time. "Where's that blue paint? You said it was in the kitchen, but I didn't see it anywhere. And where's Mr. Quigley?"

Urging her forward, Jacob said resolutely, "To the parlor, Elizabeth. No more questions."

Her thoughts were in a whirl trying to sort out the answers, but she pushed them aside when she paused in front of the parlor door. As she stood facing the pretty varnished oak panels, the sun came out, sending warm light through the entryway to highlight the rich grain. Putting her hand on the porcelain knob, she realized all was silent—too silent. Slowly, she turned the handle.

CHAPTER

15

"Surprise!" a chorus of voices sounded forth.

Suddenly, Elizabeth was facing an assembly of familiar faces—Mr. Quigley, the Clarkes, Farrels, Sayers, Langtons, Knights, along with Louisa and Jeremy. Behind her neighbors was a collection of household items—chairs, a settee, and lanterns. Naomi, Phoebe, Jane, and Ruth were closest to her, and at their feet was a handsome cradle.

"Mrs. Morgan, this is our special gift for you!" said Naomi, her hand on the cradle top. "My papa made this." She rocked it back and forth.

"This is truly lovely!" said Elizabeth, running her hand over the smooth finish. The piece displayed the same skilled craftsmanship as in the rocking chair Mr. Farrell had made for her.

Jane Langton removed the baby quilt from the rocker and held it up, revealing its pastel sunshine and shadow pattern in its entirety. "Ruth and I pieced this together," she said.

"And Phoebe and her mama quilted it," added Ruth.

Elizabeth took ahold of the soft cover, admiring its fine stitching. "You've done a splendid job, all of you."

Naomi removed the pad from the cradle. "And I made this so your baby will have somethin' real soft to lie on."

Squeezing the cotton-filled muslin, Elizabeth said, "I'm

sure my baby will spend many comfortable hours in this cradle, thanks to you, Naomi."

In the quiet moment that followed, the unmistakable whistle of the *Governor Marcy* could be heard.

"I'd better get down to the dock!" Dr. Brownell told Elizabeth. "It's Captain Winthrop with the rest of your furniture—the things I brought from Brockport—and I don't want them getting broken when they're delivered!"

"Come on, fellows, we've got a job to do," said Jacob, retrieving his coat from the entryway floor.

"Jacob, you told me the *Governor Marcy* was leaving Upper Saginaw *tomorrow*," Elizabeth reminded him.

He offered a guilty smile. "I misled you. It was the only way I could carry out this ruse without your knowledge. Will you forgive me?"

"Of course," she said affectionately.

He kissed her cheek. "I've got to go. I've hired Mr. Cromwell's ox and oxcart to bring everything from our cabin, and from the dock once the *Governor Marcy* has been unloaded. We'll be back soon with the first delivery. All you have to do is tell us where to put everything." He hurried out the door.

When all the men had hustled off, Louisa said to the women, "Ladies, we've got our own job to do, puttin' on the midday meal. We'd best go and fetch them vittles we been keepin' warm on our hearths." To Elizabeth, she said, "We'll be back in two shakes of a lamb's tail. You just keep the fire burnin', and we'll take care of the rest. This is gonna be the finest dinner in Riverton since last summer, when we fixed up that cabin for ya." Taking Jeremy by the hand, she said, "Come on, son. We've gotta go home and feed Blackfoot, and fetch our dinner."

"Louisa, wait!" Elizabeth caught her by the arm. "You don't mean to serve a meal *here*, do you?"

"Why not?"

"Why not?" Jeremy echoed his mother.

"Because . . . I don't even have a dining table, let alone enough chairs to seat everybody!"

"I see table. I see chairs," insisted Jeremy.

"Where are they?" Elizabeth asked the boy.

"In there!" Jeremy grasped the knob of the dining room door with both hands and opened it.

Inside, makeshift sawhorse tables and benches had been set for dinner, but the real centerpiece of the room was the large oak table by the bay window. Elizabeth stepped between the matching oak chairs to admire the tabletop, its honey-gold finish reflecting the light from the window. Its beauty, and remarkable similarity to the dining suite in her father's house, took her breath away.

Louisa and Jeremy came beside her. "There's been a whole passel of activity here you didn't know nothin'—anything—about, ever since we learned your papa was comin' to Riverton to stay. Now you'd best sit down in one of your new chairs and contemplate that while the rest of us womenfolk get on about our chores!" Heading out the door, she called back over her shoulder, "And keep that kitchen hearth warm while we're gone. We're gonna need it!"

"I will!" Elizabeth promised. When the door had closed behind Louisa, the silence was almost deafening. Alone in her new home, joy and thanksgiving for God's bountiful blessings filled her heart to overflowing, causing tears to roll down her face again. She patted them dry and rose from the chair.

Making her way to the kitchen, she added a couple of medium-sized pieces of pine to the fire, noticing for the first time the new andirons holding the logs, and a poker, shovel, and broom that stood in a stand beside the hearth. Taking the poker in hand, she found the initials, "I.K." on its handle. Isaac had made a truly useful and attractive contribution to her home.

While she was waiting for the new logs to catch, she inspected the varnish on the knotty pine cupboards that had been installed in the kitchen and pantry since the last time she'd been in the house. No longer would she have to store her dishes and staples on open shelves.

With the fire burning well, she returned to the parlor to take a close look at the other pieces of furniture she had only glimpsed briefly when the room had been crowded with people. A rocking settee with a place to lay the baby had been fashioned of walnut. Its dark tone stood in striking contrast to the paler maple floor and pine wainscoating. Beside it were chairs similarly made, and hanging above the fireplace was a mirror. On the walls to either side were lanterns, and two sconces holding thick, white candles ready to light up a dreary winter's eve.

She ventured upstairs. Despite the fact that Jacob had once said the second floor would have to wait a year, the master bedroom was completely ready, furnished with a canopy bed like the one she'd admired in Governor Mason's home. And beside it was a set of bed stairs with a hidden commode identical to the one Jacob had promised her!

The baby's nursery in the adjacent room had already been painted a perfect shade of sky blue, and the other two bedrooms down the hall were finished as well, if not completely furnished.

From the upstairs window, she saw the ox cart pulling up in front of the house with Mr. Quigley and her papa on either side. Jacob and the other men were pushing from behind to keep from getting stuck in the mud. It seemed odd not to see Uncle Will anywhere, but she understood his absence. Banking business was keeping him busy in Upper Saginaw most days, and when he was in Riverton, he avoided Quigley.

Alongside the ox cart came the women with their hot dishes. Elizabeth went downstairs and opened the front door for them. Jane Langton was the first to enter, carrying a towel-wrapped bundle.

"Mrs. Morgan, I've brought two batches of hot biscuits fresh from Mama's hearth," Jane said. "I'll put them in the kitchen for you."

"Thank you, Jane. I'm much obliged." A new thought came to Elizabeth, and she followed the young girl down the corridor. "Jane, have you met my papa?"

"Yes, ma'am," she grinned broadly. "I told him I want to be a medicine lady, just like you! I even asked if he would let me read his medical books, and he said I could, just as soon as he got them unpacked!" She set the biscuits on the warm hearth.

"Good! Let's go see what we can find!"

After Elizabeth had located her father's medical books, she returned to the kitchen to help the women. Louisa was in full charge, and when an opportunity arose, Elizabeth took her aside to speak with her privately. "I really appreciate all the effort you've put into this, Louisa. I only wish your husband were here, too."

Louisa wiped her hands nervously on her apron. "He

said the bankin' inspector was comin' today, and he had to stay in Upper Saginaw to meet him, but I don't believe it. Will's nursin' that grudge against Mr. Quigley, and when I said as much, we had harsh words."

Elizabeth hugged Louisa. "I'm sorry. If there's anything I can do . . . "

Louisa shook her head sadly, then a sly grin crept across her face. "I'll tell ya what ya can do. You have yourself a real nice time today, so ya can always think fondly on the day ya moved into y'r frame house."

"It's already been a day to remember!" Elizabeth assured her.

Will Morgan paced back and forth across the tiny floor of his hastily-constructed log bank, his gaze fixed on the small chest atop the counter on the teller's side of the wooden bars. For the tenth time in ten minutes, he lifted the lid of the chest, studied the gold and silver coins heaped inside, then carefully shut the cover so as not to jar the contents.

Stepping outside, he stared longingly at the tavern door of the Western Hotel across the street, sorely tempted to join the Upper Saginaw directors of the bank, who were buying rounds for the state banking inspector. Resisting the urge, he went back inside, opened the teller's drawer, and again counted each stack of crisp, new bank notes.

He had repeated the process twice more when the sound of familiar voices heralded the approach of his banking partners and their honored guest. Mr. Pierce, who had provided space for the bank on a tiny parcel of land alongside his dry goods emporium, entered first through the back door.

"Morgan, Mr. Uriah Noble has come to inspect our banking operation!" Pierce announced boldly, ushering in a man whose short stature decreased even further upon the removal of his tall beaver hat. He was followed inside by Isreal Stevens, Fred Fenmore, and James Cromwell, who filled nearly the entire back portion of the bank.

"Welcome to the Saginaw Valley Bank, Mr. Noble," said Will, extending a hand, "the finest banking institution north of Flint!"

"Pleased to make your acquaintance," said Noble. Though his diction was fairly clear, his cheeks bore an alcoholic glow. Encouraging glances from the others told Will they'd done their job, buying rounds at the tavern.

Confidently, Will proceeded. "Our bank is capitalized at $50,000, Mr. Noble, and here's the silver and gold to back it up." He carefully lifted the lid of the chest.

Taking eyeglasses from his pocket, Noble peered at the glittering coins. "Looks like sufficient funds, all right."

Through the open doorway came angry words. "Look again, Noble!" Henry Otis elbowed his way past Stevens, Fenmore, and Cromwell to yank the chest off the counter. Shards of broken glass flew across the floor, mixed with a considerable number of nails and a sparse quantity of coins. "*That's* what's backing the notes of the Saginaw Valley Bank. They're not worth the paper they're printed on!"

Will grabbed Otis by the collar. "Get out of here, and don't you ever cross my path again!" With a violent shove, he sent Otis on his way.

"This is a most unfortunate situation," Noble lamented, hastily opening the teller drawer and stuffing the banknotes into his hat. "I'm afraid I must close down this bank until sufficient coin has been put on deposit to back your institution's paper." Setting the beaver hat atop his head, he strode out the back door, mounted his horse, and galloped off.

"I'd like to wring Otis's neck," Will said, bending down to pick the gold and silver coins out of the debris.

"He's the only one in town who's been refusing to accept our notes in payment," observed Cromwell, squatting down to help Will.

Pierce added his efforts to the task. "That's because he didn't like it when he was kicked off the board of directors. He's probably been looking for a way to get even ever since."

"He's still tradin' alcohol to Brother-of-the-Wolf, too," said Cromwell. "I saw the Injun passed out behind the hotel last Saturday night. He had an empty flask in his hand, and he reeked of whiskey."

"I thought Otis would change his ways," said Will. "Now I know different."

Elizabeth was helping Louisa and Mrs. Langton clean up the kitchen after the housewarming when her aunt came in, her unsmiling expression showing an unusual amount of strain. "Isaac and the children and I are leaving now, Elizabeth. We'll see you later," she said in a flat tone.

"Are you feeling all right, Aunt Sallie? You look tired."

Sallie put her hand to her stomach. "I'm afraid I'm feeling a bit off."

"Would you like some stomach powders? I'll get Papa to unpack them for you," Elizabeth offered, hanging her dish rag over the side of the wash basin.

"No, thank you," Sallie said curtly. "I'll be fine."

"I'll be glad to make ya some chamomile tea," Louisa offered, pulling out a chair. "Why don't ya set yourself down and rest a spell. It's been a long day."

"I said I'll be fine," Sallie repeated irritably. "I have to go now. Isaac and the children are waiting for me out front."

Elizabeth walked her aunt to the front door. "Thanks so much for helping with everything, Aunt Sallie. This has been a wonderful day."

Dr. Brownell came up behind Elizabeth. "Yes, thanks, Sallie. You've been a real help." To Elizabeth, he said, "I rode the *Governor Marcy* to Upper Saginaw and walked here a few days ago, just so you wouldn't see me getting off at Will's dock. Ever since, I've been helping Jacob finish the house, and your aunt has been bringing me my meals." He bent to kiss Sallie's cheek, but she backed away.

"It was nothing. I've got to go. Good bye," she said, hurrying out the door.

"I can't understand what's gotten into her," said Dr. Brownell. "She hasn't been herself at all these last couple of days."

"It was probably just the strain of planning such big doings," Elizabeth reasoned. "She said her stomach was off. If you'll get me some stomach powders, I'll take them to her as soon as the other guests have gone."

"I'll see what I can find," her father promised.

An hour later, while Jacob helped her father with his unpacking, Elizabeth set out for the Knights' smithy. Dusk was settling over the river when she knocked on the back door and Isaac answered.

"I've brought some stomach powders for Aunt Sallie,"

Elizabeth said. "Is she feeling any better?"

Lines of bewilderment wrinkled his forehead. "She's out walking Rascal. You'll probably find her down by the river."

"Thanks, Isaac. I'll look there." Elizabeth took the steps to the dock, then spotted her aunt and the dog going down the path several yards north of the blockhouse. "Aunt Sallie!" her voice echoed over the still water.

Sallie waved and started toward her. Rascal bounded ahead of her mistress, greeting Elizabeth with happy yaps, her tail wagging fiercely. Elizabeth spoke to the dog in calm tones, quieting her by the time Sallie joined them.

"Here are the stomach powders," Elizabeth said, offering her aunt the paper packet.

Sallie's hand trembled when she took the the small parcel from Elizabeth and tucked it into her skirt pocket. "I'm afraid I'll have to move away from Riverton. This place doesn't seem to be agreeing with me anymore," she said, signs of strain still obvious on her face.

"Papa says you haven't been yourself for a couple of days, now. Is that right?"

A silent moment followed, and even in the dim light, Elizabeth could see her aunt's eyes filling with tears. "I just can't . . . stay here anymore. Not now that . . . " She turned away, dabbing her eyes with her handkerchief.

"I don't understand," said Elizabeth, caressing her aunt's shoulder. "I thought you and Isaac were happy here."

"He is," she said shortly. "I was too . . . until . . . " She began to cry, her sobs muffled by the linen cloth.

Elizabeth put her arm about her aunt, a new thought coming to her. "Aunt Sallie, you never told me why you left Brockport all those years ago, except that it had to do with Papa. Now that he's here, you want to leave again. Please tell me what the trouble is between you."

Sallie gained control of herself and faced Elizabeth. "I've been a fool with a fancy for your father. That's the trouble."

A stunned silence followed, then Sallie continued. "I left Brockport when I realized your father would never return my feelings. As long as I was away from him, I managed to get on all right. But now he's here, and I'm . . . falling apart. I feel so *guilty!*" Her eyes began to well with tears again.

Elizabeth embraced her aunt, completely at a loss for words.

Moments later, Sallie drew away, in tenuous control of herself again. "Elizabeth, I want you to know I love Isaac. Please don't ever speak a word of this to him. He's a good husband and a wonderful father. I couldn't bear to hurt him!"

"Of course not," Elizabeth replied.

"I've got to put the past behind me," Sallie fretted. "I just don't know how!"

In a moment of inspiration, Elizabeth asked, "Have you sought God's help?"

Sallie nodded. "I've prayed and prayed. It hasn't done me a bit of good."

"I'm going to pray for you, too, starting now." Elizabeth bowed her head. "Dear Heavenly Father, please help Aunt Sallie put her feelings in order so that she can be happy again. In Jesus' name, Amen."

Sallie offered a doubtful look. "That would be a miracle."

"Then you should expect a miracle," Elizabeth said.

"Don't lose faith, and don't stop praying. I believe deep in my heart, God is going to answer you."

Sallie sighed. "In the meantime, don't be offended if I keep my distance from your new house."

"I won't," Elizabeth promised, offering an understanding smile.

CHAPTER

16

Will stepped into the back corner of the blockhouse, lifted the basket of dried whitefish onto his shoulder, then raised his lantern and took inventory of the remaining supplies. Less than fifty pounds of buckwheat remained. The flour had run out weeks ago, cornmeal had disappeared this week, and no one in Riverton had tasted a piece of dried fruit or a vegetable in the last two months.

Christmas had been bleak, and would have been bleaker except that he and Walks Tall had been able to shoot the last two deer to be seen in the area. Since then, no big game had been taken by anyone in Riverton or the Chippewa village, and only a few small animals had turned up in the traps. The howl of a wolf, and the answer echoing in the distance reminded Will of the hungry packs which had stolen from many of the traps and had run down dozens of deer, leaving nothing but hair, hooves, and picked-over skeletons.

A chill ran up his spine, and he knew it wasn't just the sound of the wolves, or the whistling of the wind making him shudder, but the thought that despite careful rationing, his community would soon be starving. The Chippewa village was no better off. If only the *Governor Marcy* had been able to make it up the Saginaw River to deliver its last load before winter set in, both villages could have been spared the suffering.

But the early onset of cold weather had forced the steamer to turn back to Desmond, or Port Huron as it had been recently renamed. Eighty-five miles separated Riverton from the much-needed staples—eighty-five miles of frozen swamp and woods, and trails knee- to waist-deep in drifted snow.

He stepped outside, the night wind nearly whipping his foxtail hat off his head as he bolted and locked the door. With labored strides, he made his way through the deep drifts of snow, the hooting of an owl haunting him as he climbed up the riverbank and tried to follow his own filled-in tracks back to the cabin.

Across the way, a light shown in Quigley's place. It seemed ironic to have him back in the same cabin he'd occupied as a squatter. If the bank hadn't failed, leaving Will with engraver's bills, and desperately short of cash, he'd never have agreed to sell a square inch of Riverton to the scoundrel. But seeing as how Quigley had already gained deed to the parcels adjoining Jacob's property on the south, there seemed no good reason not to deal with the man. He was the only person hereabouts that possessed cash money, and he was the only one who knew that Will's story about Mr. LaMore had been completely made up. So Will had conveniently added to the lie, saying LaMore had requested him to sell the cabin for the best price.

Will hadn't forgiven Quigley for past transgressions, though. Anger over losing Grandpa Morgan's diaries would remain in Will's heart until he went to his grave. He put those thoughts aside as he reached his own cabin, stomped the snow from his boots, and brushed the layer of white stuff from his shoulders and cap before stepping indoors.

Louisa was sitting by the fire, a thick shawl wrapped about her shoulders and a deerskin lap robe covering her skirt as she knitted a pair of baby booties. As if food wasn't short enough, she was gaining in appetite every day in anticipation of the birth of their first child in June, and Will worried that she was giving her own portions to Jeremy whenever he complained of hunger. She put down her knitting and came to inspect the basket he planted on the table.

"There's no more meat?" she asked quietly so as not to wake the sleeping boy.

"No meat, and no fish but what's in that basket," Will said, taking off his cap and coat and hanging them on the wall. When he turned to Louisa again, she was looking at the fish with a watery-eyed gaze.

"There ain't gonna be but a scrap of fish apiece, by the time we divvy it up for every family in town," she half-whispered.

Will could only stare at the basket, thinking how close he'd come to refusing it when the Chief had offered it to him last August. He took Louisa gently by the shoulder, tipping her chin to gaze directly into her tear-stained face. "Don't you fret, now. It's not good for the baby. I'll get a deer this week. I just know it."

Louisa shook her head. "No ya won't. You're a right good hunter, but ya haven't even seen tracks in over a month." She blotted her tears with her apron and swallowed hard. "Captain Langton's gonna have to butcher that cow you and Jacob are sharin' with him. That's what it comes down to," she said in a trembling voice.

"No! I won't have him making a meal of Saucy!"

"But the Captain said there's hardly any feed left. She'll starve, too, 'less we do somethin'!"

Will clenched his fists, frustration and anger surging deep within. Then he took a deep breath and pulled out a couple of chairs. "Sit down, Louisa. I want to talk to you." When she'd done as he said, he sat facing her, taking both of her hands in his. "I'm going to Upper Saginaw in the morning to see Cromwell. I'll arrange for two pair of his of oxen and two sleds. Then I'll come back and make up a party of rugged men—some from Riverton and some from the Chippewa village—and we'll go to Desmond to bring back the supplies from the *Governor Marcy*."

Louisa pulled away. "Are you outta your mind? That's miles and miles from here. You'll never make it. Not the way it's been snowin' this winter."

Will slammed his fist against the table. "If my Grandpa Morgan could go three hundred miles in the snow to bring artillery from Fort Ticonderoga to Boston in the winter of '76, then surely, I can go eighty-five miles to get the supplies that will keep my village, and the Indians from starving!"

Elizabeth climbed into bed while Jacob stoked the fire one last time. Come tomorrow morning, she would be alone in the room. She shoved aside thoughts of Jacob's early morning departure for Port Huron, thinking instead of the young governor who'd written her father and helped convince him to come to Michigan. She wondered if it had been a blessing, or a curse. They'd never expected to be facing hunger during their first winter in the Saginaw Valley.

The fire crackled softly, and the faint odor of smoke

tinged the air as Jacob laid a sizable stick of hardwood atop a glowing log. He draped his robe over his valet stand and climbed in beside her, wrapping his arm about her and holding her close, then running his hand across her swollen belly.

The baby kicked, and she knew he felt it too. He nuzzled her ear, whispering, "I love you, Elizabeth. Take good care of our baby while I'm gone."

She took his hand in hers, kissing his knuckles. "I love you, too, Jacob. Promise you'll be careful."

"Of course," Jacob said, kissing her nose. "Promise you'll pray for us."

"I'll be praying every minute until you're home again," she said. Then, she began to tremble, worry and tears overwhelming her. Jacob tightened his embrace. A few minutes later, when she had gained control of herself, she whispered, "Your love has made me more happy than words can say. I know you have to go away, but I hate thinking I might lose you."

"Then don't think of it, my darling. Hold my love in your heart, and believe in my promise to return just as soon as I can."

The morning sky was still dark when Jacob slipped out of bed, stoked the fire, and made ready to join Isaac, his uncle, and Walks Tall. When he had dressed, he paused by the bed to gaze at Elizabeth one last time, cherishing the sight of her in her ruffled nightcap, sleeping peacefully beneath the down comforter. He brushed her cheek with a kiss and hurried downstairs, knowing that lingering only amplified the pain of parting.

In the back room, he pulled his pack on over his

shoulders. When he stepped outside, the bitter cold almost numbed his fingers before he had fastened his snowshoes to his boots. Pulling on his fur-lined mittens, he took off across the newfallen snow. The wind had subsided, the sky had cleared, and the ground glistened in the moonbeams. It would almost seem pretty, if circumstances weren't so grave.

All was quiet as he headed for Will and Louisa's cabin. When he reached the smithy, Isaac joined him, no words being necessary as they made their way across waves of snowdrifts. A couple of minutes later, Jacob heard voices in the distance muffled by the blanket of snow. As he neared Will and Louisa's cabin, he saw that the two teams of oxen were already yoked and hitched to sleds, and that Quigley and Brother-of-the-Wolf were talking with his uncle and Walks Tall.

"I know the trails to Desmond better than any white man in Michigan," Quigley claimed. "And Brother-of-the-Wolf is the finest Chippewa hunter in these parts. Ya know y'r gonna have to have some game to keep ya alive. You're foolish to go without us, Will Morgan!"

"I'd be foolish to let you come!" Will argued. "Brother-of-the-Wolf turns to whiskey whenever the spirit moves, and Walks Tall is the best guide, bar none. I'm warning you both to keep your distance!"

Brother-of-the-Wolf stepped forward, his arms crossed against his chest as he gazed directly at Will. "Four moons passed. Brother-of-the-Wolf drink no whiskey. Me drink no whiskey forever."

"He's tellin' the truth," said Quigley. "He hasn't touched alcohol since last October."

Will picked his rifle up from the sled. "And I'm telling

you one last time, I don't need your help. Now get out of my sight, both of you."

Quigley spoke to Brother-of-the-Wolf in Chippewa, and the two of them left without further objections.

Will set his rifle on the sled again and turned to Isaac and Jacob. "Let's get moving. We've got a long way to go before we bed down for the night. Walks Tall says the best place is nearly fifteen miles from here."

Fierce wind whipped powder-light snow into whorls and sheets. Even on quieter days, Jacob hadn't been able to see much of a trail, snowbound as it had been, but somehow they'd made the journey to Port Huron and three-quarters of the way back. Now, in the fading light of a late winter afternoon, a blizzard was moving in, and he felt as though his eyes were about to freeze over. With the thumb of his mitten, he brushed the ice crystals off his eyelashes and plodded ahead, leading the second yoke of oxen in the path behind Will and Walks Tall's team. Their destination was an abandoned cabin about seven miles ahead, and he wondered whether he could make it there before his fingers and toes suffered frostbite. He prayed silently each step of the way, asking God to keep his circulation moving.

While his feet moved forward, his thoughts and prayers reflected on the miles that had already passed. He thanked the Lord for the wild game that had turned up dead in their path each day of the southward trek. He was sure Quigley and Brother-of-the-Wolf had been staying close-by, leaving the dead rabbits where they'd be sure to find them. With the supplies from the *Governor Marcy* aboard the sleds, food was no longer a problem, but the wolves had become increasingly bold at night. The scent of the provisions drew them in packs, and they would circle around the encampment, snuffing and growling hungrily. Only the bright firelight kept them at bay.

Will's voice interrupted the thought as he shouted to his team, taking them off the trail and into a partial clearing. Jacob followed his lead, bringing his own team alongside. Isaac came up from his position at the rear.

Will plodded over to them, his beard, fur hat, and collar thick with snow. "The weather's getting worse. Walks Tall says we can't make it to the cabin. We need to build a shelter for the night. He's gone to cut some hemlock boughs. Isaac, help me gather wood for a fire. Jacob, keep watch of things."

Jacob nodded, and loaded his rifle as a precaution. To keep his blood moving, he walked a circular path around the two teams and sleds, watching for any sign of predators. On his third time around, the oxen started to shift nervously in their yokes. In the distance, a huge gray wolf slunk through the trees.

"Heeyah!" Jacob shouted. "Get out of here!" He raised his rifle and took aim. When he pulled the trigger, the cap burst, but the shot didn't go off. The wolf started directly for him. With no time to reload, Jacob tossed aside his rifle and pulled out his hunting knife. His movement hampered by snowshoes, he took a stance, his heart pounding.

With a low growl, the animal drew near, his vaporous breath escaping through two rows of fangs. The creature lunged. With an upward cut, Jacob plunged his knife into the wolf's throat the way Brother-of-the-Wolf had taught him on their hunting trips.

The weight of the animal knocked Jacob back. A shot rang out. Jacob's head hit the side of the sled. His world went dark.

Jeremy and the four Knight children—along with Black-foot and Rascal—were playing games on the parlor floor while Elizabeth sat with Louisa and Sallie by the fire tending her knitting. The day after Jacob had left for Port Huron, Elizabeth had invited the others to move in with her until the men's return. Sallie had come only reluctantly, but the situation was made more tenable by Dr. Brownell's penchant for spending evenings alone in the study he'd set up in one corner of the dining room, reading his medical books. Elizabeth said a silent prayer of thanks that except for occasional sibling spats, time was passing tolerably well on these worry-filled nights of waiting.

Food was at a premium. The weather had turned stormy, and the men had been gone a full four days longer than the two weeks they had predicted. Meals had become increasingly skimpy. Wolf meat offered little appeal, but somehow, Elizabeth managed to find a way to prepare it. And every evening she served half a slice of buckwheat bread for each child as a bedtime snack. Given with a few swallows of warm milk, it helped the children to sleep better, and Elizabeth went to the kitchen now to prepare the scant meal.

Sallie joined her, filling five cups with a portion of milk while Elizabeth sliced the bread and spread it with a thin coat of Saucy's butter. When they had set the table with the cups and the plate of bread, Sallie caught Elizabeth's hand in hers.

"We hardly get two seconds alone together," she said, "but I wanted to tell you something before we call in the children."

Elizabeth squeezed Sallie's hand encouragingly.

Her aunt's eyes grew watery as she continued. "I'm not sure if the bad weather is a curse, or a blessing, but one thing I've learned since Isaac left . . . " When she continued, her voice was but a whisper. "I sure do love that man more than I ever realized!" A tear trickled down her cheek. She dashed it dry with the back of her hand. "I don't know what I'm going to do if anything happens to him!" she said in a broken voice.

A lump clogged Elizabeth's throat. She swallowed hard and spoke past it. "Nothing's going to happen to him," she said in a half-whisper. "Isaac and Jacob will be home any day now, and we'll all sit down to a feast. I promise!"

"I pray to God you're right," said Sallie, blowing her nose into her handkerchief before calling the children to the table.

Hours later, long after Elizabeth had gone to bed, she lay awake fretting. "Dear Lord, I beg you to stop the snowstorm, and bring Jacob and Isaac and the others home tomorrow," she prayed earnestly. "I can't stand the worry anymore. My hope is running out, just like the food. The buckwheat is nearly gone, now . . . but You already know that. *Please,* Lord, bring us our husbands, and the supplies we need to stay alive!"

A moment later, she felt pain in her abdomen. She lay still until the contraction passed, and two more had come and gone. Then she got up, put on her wrapper, and went down the hall to wake her papa.

"Darius Jacob Morgan, will you ever know your papa?" Elizabeth asked her two-day-old baby as she rocked him in her favorite chair. He quickly fell asleep in her arms. She considered laying him in his cradle, but she couldn't bear to put him down.

Her gaze fell on the canopy bed. How she hated the loneliness of sleeping there without Jacob. The prayer she had said a hundred times in recent days came silently and automatically to mind. *Dear Lord, please bring Jacob home today!*

Fatigue overcame her as it often did during late afternoon, and her eyes drifted shut. In her semi-sleepy state, a familiar nightmarish vision of Jacob in the wilderness haunted her. It was the same horrible dream she'd had time and time again since he'd left home. He was injured and unable to get up from a snowdrift. She reached out to him, and he to her. Just when their hands were about to meet, his image would always fade to white—a mirage—and she would wake up. This time, his image remained vivid and his hand clasped hers, warm and comforting.

Her eyes blinked open, and there was Jacob smiling broadly, his hand enveloping hers as he knelt beside her.

"Elizabeth, my darling!" He pressed his lips to hers, his kiss tasting sweeter than any she'd known. A moment later, he gazed lovingly at his son. "He's perfect, just as I knew he would be."

As Jacob gently stroked Darius's cheek, Elizabeth couldn't help noticing the deep scratches on his own face. "You've been hurt," she said, caressing his stubbly chin.

Jacob brought her hands to his lips and kissed her fingertips. "A wolf attacked me, but Brother-of-the-Wolf killed him before any real harm came. Thanks to him and Mr. Quigley, we all made it back safely with the provisions."

Elizabeth blinked back the tears that were starting to form. "I love you so much, Jacob, I couldn't bear the thought of losing you. Thank God, my prayers are answered, and you're here, beside me!"

He kissed her nose, her cheeks, her lips. "Elizabeth, my love, I pray I'll never have to leave you again!"

CHAPTER

17

Will watched the huge sign "LAND AUCTION JUNE 23" flap against the side of the blockhouse that would soon belong to someone else. The riverbank between Isaac's smithy and the dock had been jammed since ten in the morning with every able-bodied soul in the county eager to see who would buy the better part of his Riverton section for unpaid taxes. Standing back from the crowd, Will listened while the auctioneer read the surveyor's description of the last parcel up for sale—the blockhouse, dock, and surrounding property. When the bidding started, this prime location went the way all the previous parcels had gone. Early bids were quickly surpassed by offers from Quigley.

"Going once . . . going twice . . . sold to the man in the red shirt!"

The crack of the wooden gavel against the podium sent one last current of resentment coursing through Will's veins. Quigley had bought it all—every last piece of property Will owned, except for Louisa's cabin. As the crowd disbursed, he hurried across the settlement for home where his wife was waiting with their one-day-old daughter to learn the results of the bidding. How ironic, he thought, that just when his homelife was more satisfying than ever, his fortune in the Saginaw Valley had turned to ruins. The part that troubled him most was that for the life of him, he couldn't figure out how the cabinetmaker from Detroit had amassed enough hard cash to start building a church and schoolhouse on the lots Jacob had deeded him, and to buy all of the property that had come up for auction.

Four hours after the auction had ended, Will felt desperately in need of solitude. He paddled his canoe to the shore of the narrow island in the center of the river, took out his fishing pole, and began casting his baited hook into the water. His mind was still numb from the auction. Under normal circumstances, he would have sought refuge in the loft of his blockhouse, but that was no longer an option. He needed time to grow accustomed to the fact that someone else owned it now, along with the other land in the Riverton section he had called his own until today.

Again and again, he tossed his bait into the river. The plunking sound held solace, as did the rat-a-tat-tat of a nearby woodpecker. He tried to think what he should do with his life now. For four years, he had invested heart, soul, and capital into the Saginaw Valley. Now, he felt empty inside, drained dry of finances and feelings. The cost of printing bank notes, and the bills for the supplies he'd brought back from the *Governor Marcy* last winter had eaten up his cash. The Riverton folks had done what they could to help pay for the food that had kept them alive, but when taxes came due, there was only enough money for the half-acre plot where Louisa's cabin stood.

He was wondering what new direction his life should take when he noticed a canoe approaching from the opposite shore. As it drew near, he recognized Quigley's hefty profile.

Will sighed. Casting his line, he waited until the intruder was closer to shore to register his dismay.

"The fish aren't biting here, Quigley. Why don't you go back where you came from?" Will's gravelly voice reverberated across the quiet water.

"I didn't come for the fishin', Morgan, and I don't think you did either. We gotta talk."

"We've got nothing to say to each other." Will cast his line again.

Quigley pulled his canoe up beside Will's and climbed out. "Speak for yourself, Morgan. I got somethin' important to tell ya." He pulled a sheaf of papers from inside his shirt and tossed them into the bottom of Will's canoe. "Those are your deeds. I don't want 'em." A moment later, he started to push his canoe into the water again.

"Wait up, Quigley." Will set down his pole and picked up the deeds. Sure enough, they were all there. His heart thumped hard. He focused on Quigley's craggy face. "Why?"

"God." A peaceful look came over the cabinetmaker that made Will envious.

"I don't understand."

Quigley smiled. "Lord knows, I'd be more 'n happy to explain it to ya." He gestured toward a grassy knoll.

Will stuffed the deeds into his own shirt and sat down beside Quigley.

"Let me tell ya a story 'bout my family," he began. "My great-grandpappy was nothin' like your grandpappy who fought the war. Long ago, he made himself real rich in one of the ugliest businesses a man could enter—the slave trade. Back when it was still legal, he was part owner in a slaver with a Britisher, name of John Newton. Ever heard of him?"

213

Will thought a moment. "Don't believe I ever did."

"Well, after Mr. Newton was in the slave trade awhile, his conscience got the best of him. He quit and became a minister. He had a real gift with words, too. I'll sing ya a song he wrote." Quigley began a little off key.

> Amazing grace! how sweet the sound,
> That saved a wretch like me!
> I once was lost, but now am found
> Was blind, but now I see.

Quigley's eyes had misted over, and Will could see that he was struggling to maintain control. As silent moments passed, he pondered the words of the song, and realized for quite some time, he'd been blind to many things, including the good in Quigley.

The cabinetmaker continued in a voice made husky by emotion. "When the family fortune came to me, I was ashamed. I wondered why my great-grandpappy couldn't have done like John Newton did.

"Years passed. Angry years. Then I moved to the Saginaw Valley and married White Dove. I was happy for the first time in a long while. I decided to spend some of my inheritance on land here. When you bought the Riverton section out from under me, my old anger flared up. I went into a rage and set your cabin on fire. It upset White Dove so, she delivered before her time had come. When she and the baby died, my world seemed black.

"Then God taught me a wonderful lesson. He laid me on my back with cholera and sent Father Kundig to show me how to make my life really count for somethin'. I've been listenin' to God ever since, tryin' to help where I can."

Looking Will straight in the eye, he said, "God sent me up here to help you, Will Morgan, and to do somethin' honorable with my money."

Will's throat grew tight. With an effort, he said, "How can I thank you?"

Quigley smiled. His hand on Will's shoulder, he said simply, "By thankin' God."

Eight days later, exactly one year after Elizabeth and Jacob had arrived in Riverton, she was standing beside her husband at the makeshift altar of the newly framed-in church, cringing at the sound of her son's lusty cry. The moment she'd transferred him to Reverend Clarke's arms to be baptized, he'd been voicing his discontent, and it grew louder when the minister dipped his fingertips into the bowl of water and touched them to the infant's forehead.

"Darius Jacob Morgan, I baptize thee in the name of the Father, and of the Son, and of the Holy Ghost. Amen." The reverend settled the protesting infant back in his mother's arms.

Elizabeth rocked him back and forth. "Shhh. Shhh, Darius," she whispered as the minister offered another prayer. But Darius's bawling remained boisterous, and when Reverend Clarke was ready to continue with the regular church service, she carried the baby outside.

Jacob followed them to the shade of a spreading oak in the front yard. Gazing at his son, his mouth curved in a wry smile. "If anyone in Riverton considered skipping Sunday services to sleep late, they're surely awake by now."

Elizabeth focused on the church, its congregation visible through the open, upright beams. "From the looks of it, the whole town showed up for church today, and half the Chippewa village, as well."

"It's quite a blessing, seeing the Lord's house nearly full for the first services to be held beneath the new roof," Jacob observed. "Of course, the biggest blessing for me, is seeing Mr. Quigley sitting in the same pew with my uncle. I'm glad they've become friends."

Elizabeth shifted Darius to her shoulder and patted his back. Moments later, when he'd grown quiet, she spoke softly. "Four months ago, I'd never have expected to see Uncle Will in Mr. Quigley's company by choice."

In the distance, the congregation could be heard singing *Amazing Grace*, Mr. Quigley's favorite hymn, and Jacob's as well. He listened carefully to the words about dangers, toils, and snares, and silently thanked God for keeping him and his loved ones safe from the perils of the wilderness.

He turned Elizabeth toward him, his heart overflowing with love for the woman he adored and the son she had given him, more precious than life itself. God's grace had been abundant beyond words!

Elizabeth gazed into Jacob's blue-as-the-river eyes, so full of affection for her and Darius, she could sense it surrounding them both. When his lips lightly touched hers, she knew it was his wordless promise that no matter what their future in Riverton should bring, with God's help, and their love for one another, they would see it through.

ABOUT DONNA WINTERS

Donna adopted Michigan as her home state in 1971 when she moved there from a small town outside of Rochester, New York. She began penning novels in 1982 while working full time for an electronics company in Grand Rapids.

She resigned in 1984 following a contract offer for her first book. Since then, she has written several romance novels for various publishers, including Thomas Nelson Publishers, Zondervan Publishing House, and Guideposts.

Her husband, Fred, an American History teacher, shares her enthusiasm for history. Together, they visit historical sites, restored villages, museums, and lake ports, purchasing books and reference materials for use in Donna's research and Fred's classroom. A trip to the Bay County Historical Society's library and gift shop provided her with much of the background information for *Elizabeth of Saginaw Bay.*

Donna has lived all of her life in states bordering on the Great Lakes. Her familiarity and fascination with these remarkable inland waters and her residence in the heart of Great Lakes Country make her the perfect candidate for writing *Great Lakes Romances*®. (Photo by Renee Werni.)

Mackinac
by
Donna Winters
First in the series of *Great Lakes Romances*
(Set at Grand Hotel, Mackinac Island, 1895)
*Her name bespeaks the age in which she
lives* . . .but **Victoria Whitmore** is no shy, retiring Victorian miss. She finds herself aboard the *Algomah*, traveling from staid Grand Rapids to Michigan's fashionable Mackinac Island resort. Her journey is not one of pleasure; a restful holiday does not await her. Mackinac's Grand Hotel owes the Whitmores money—enough to save the furniture manufactory from certain financial ruin. It becomes Victoria's mission to venture to the island to collect the payment. At Mackinac, however, her task is anything but easy, and she finds more than she bargained for.

Rand Bartlett, the hotel manager, is part of that bargain. Accustomed to challenges and bent on making the struggling Grand a success, he has not counted on the challenge of Victoria—and he certainly has not counted on losing his heart to her.

The Captain and the Widow
by
Donna Winters
Second in the series of *Great Lakes Romances*
(Set in Chicago, South Haven, and
Mackinac Island, 1897)
*Lily Atwood Haynes is beautiful, intelligent, and
ahead of her time* . . . but even her grit and determination

have not prepared her for the cruel event on Lake Michigan that leaves her widowed at age twenty. It is the lake—with its fathomless depths and unpredictable forces—that has provided her livelihood. Now it is the lake that challenges her newfound happiness.

When **Captain Hoyt Curtiss**, her husband's best friend, steps in to offer assistance in navigating the choppy waters of Lily's widowhood, she can only guess at the dark secret that shrouds his past and chokes his speech. What kind of miracle will it take to forge a new beginning for *The Captain and the Widow*? *Note:* The Captain and the Widow *is a spin-off from* Mackinac.

Sweethearts of Sleeping Bear Bay
by
Donna Winters
Third in the series of *Great Lakes Romances*
(Set in the Sleeping Bear Dune region of
northern Michigan, 1898)

Mary Ellen Jenkins is a woman of rare courage and experience . . . One of only four females licensed as navigators and steamboat masters on the Western Rivers, she is accustomed to finding her way through dense fog on the Mississippi. But when she travels North for the first time in her twenty-nine years, she discovers herself unprepared for the havoc caused by a vaporous shroud off Sleeping Bear Point. And navigating the misty shoals of her own uncertain future poses an even greater threat to her peace of mind.

Self-confident, skilled, and devoted to his duties as Second Mate aboard the Lake Michigan sidewheeler, *Lily Belle,* **Thad Grant** regrets his promise to play escort to the petticoat navigator the instant he lays eyes on her plain face. Then his career runs aground. Can he trust this woman to guide him to safe harbor, or will the Lady Reb ever be able to overcome the great gulf between them?

Note: Sweethearts of Sleeping Bear Bay *is a spin-off from* The Captain and the Widow.

Charlotte of South Manitou Island
by
Donna Winters
Fourth in the series of *Great Lakes Romances*
(Set on South Manitou Island,
Michigan, 1891-1898)

Charlotte Richards' carefree world turns upside down on her eleventh birthday . . . the day her beloved papa dies in a spring storm on Lake Michigan. Without the persistence of fifteen-year-old **Seth Trevelyn,** son of South Manitou Island's lightkeeper, she might never have smiled again. He shows her that life goes on, and so does true friendship.

When Charlotte's teacher invites her to the World's Columbian Exposition of 1893, Seth signs as crewman on the *Martha G.,* carrying them to Chicago. Together, Seth and Charlotte sail the waters of the Great Lake to the very portal of the Fair, and an adventure they will never forget. While there, Seth saves Charlotte from a near fatal accident. Now, seventeen and a man, he realizes his friendship has become something more. Will his feelings be returned when Charlotte grows to womanhood?

Aurora of North Manitou Island
by
Donna Winters
Fifth in the series of *Great Lakes Romances*
(Set on North Manitou Island,
Michigan, 1898-1899)

Aurora's wedding Day was far from the glorious event she had anticipated when she put the final stitches in her white satin gown, not with her new husband lying helpless after an accident on stormy Lake Michigan. And when Serilda Anders appeared out of Harrison's past to tend the light and nurse him back to health, Aurora was certain her marriage was doomed before it had ever been properly launched.

Maybe Cad Blackburn was the answer—Cad of the ready wit and the silver tongue. But it wasn't right to accept the safe harbor *he* was offering.

Where was the light that would guide her through these troubled waters?

Bridget of Cat's Head Point
by
Donna Winters
Sixth in the series of *Great Lakes Romances*
(Set in Traverse City and the Leelanau Peninsula of Michigan, 1899-1900)

When Bridget Richards leaves South Manitou Island to take up residence on Michigan's mainland, she suffers no lack of ardent suitors. Only days after the loss of his first wife, Nat Trevelyn, Bridget's closest friend and the father of a two-year-old son, wants desperately to make her his bride. Kenton McCune, a handsome, wealthy lawyer in Traverse City, showers her with kindness the likes of which she's never known before. And Erik Olson, the son of her employer in Omena, shows her not only the incomparable beauty and romance of a Leelanau summer, but a bravery and affection beyond expectation.

Who will succeed in winning her heart? Or will tragedy swiftly intervene to steal away the promise of lasting happiness and true love?

(Note: The fourth, fifth, and sixth books in the series constitute a trilogy about three sisters in a lightkeeping family in northern Michigan.)

Jenny of L'Anse Bay
by
Donna Winters
Special Edition in the series of
Great Lakes Romances
(Set in the Keweenaw Peninsula of
Upper Michigan in 1867)

A raging fire destroys more than Jennifer Crawford's new home . . . it also burns a black hole into her future. To soothe Jennifer's resentful spirit, her parents send her on a trip with their pastor and his wife to the Indian mission at L'Anse Bay. In the wilderness of Michigan's Upper Peninsula, Jennifer soon moves from tourist to teacher, taking over the education of the Ojibway children. Without knowing their language, she must teach them English, learn their customs, and live in harmony with them.

Hawk, son of the Ojibway chief, teaches Jennifer the ways of his tribe. Often discouraged by seemingly insurmountable cultural barriers, Jennifer must also battle danger, death, and the fears that threaten to come between her and the man she loves.

Sweet Clover: A Romance of the White City
Centennial Edition in the series of
Great Lakes Romances

The World's Columbian Exposition of 1893 brought unmatched excitement and wonder to Chicago, thus inspiring this innocent tale by Clara Louise Burnham, first published in 1894.

A Chicago resident from age nine, Burnham penned her novels in an apartment overlooking Lake Michigan. Her romance books contain plots imbued with the customs and morals of a bygone era—stories that garnered a sizable, loyal readership in their day.

In *Sweet Clover*, a destitute heroine of twenty enters a marriage of convenience to ensure the security and well-being of her fatherless family. Widowed soon after, Clover Bryant Van Tassel strives to rebuild a lifelong friendship with her late husband's son. Jack Van Tassel had been her childhood playmate, and might well have become her suitor. Believing himself betrayed by both his father and the girl he once admired, Jack moves far away from his native city. Then the World's Columbian Exposition opens, luring him once again to his old family home.

Hearts warmed by friendship blossom with affection—in some most surprising ways. Will true love come to all who seek it in the Fair's fabulous White City? The author will keep you guessing till the very end!

Also by Bigwater Publishing

*Bigwater Classics*tm
A series devoted to reprinting literature of the Great Lakes that is currently unavailable to most readers

Thirty-Three Years Among the Indians
The Story of Mary Sagatoo
Edited by Donna Winters

Volume 1 in the series of *Bigwater Classics*tm

In 1863, a young woman in Massachusetts promised to marry a Chippewa Indian from the Saginaw Valley of Michigan. He was a minister whose mission was to bring Christianity to his people in the tiny Indian village of Saganing. Though he later became afflicted with consumption and learned he hadn't long to live, his betrothed would not release him from his promise of marriage. Soon after the newlyweds arrived in Michigan, this Chippewa Indian extracted a deathbed promise from his new wife.

"Mary . . . will you stay with my people, take my place among them, and try to do for them what I would have done if God had spared my life?" Joseph asked, caressing her hand.

"Oh, Joseph, don't leave me," she begged, "it is so lonesome here!"

"Please make the promise and I shall die happier. Jesus will help you keep it," he said with shortened breath.

Seeing the look of earnestness in Joseph's dark eyes, Mary replied, "I will do as you wish."

Thus began a remarkable woman's thirty-three years among a people about which she knew nothing—years of struggle, hardship, humor, and joy.

READER SURVEY—*Elizabeth of Saginaw Bay*

Your opinion counts! Please fill out and mail this form to:
Reader Survey
Bigwater Publishing
P.O. Box 177
Caledonia, MI 49316

Your
Name:_____

Street:_____

City,State,Zip:_____

In return for your completed survey, we will send you a bookmark and the latest issue of our *Great Lakes Romances Newsletter*. If your name is not currently on our mailing list, we will also include four note papers and envelopes of an historic Great Lakes scene (while supplies last).

1. Please rate the following elements from A (excellent) to E (poor).

_____Heroine   _____Hero   _____Setting   _____Plot

Comments:_____

_____

2. What setting (time and place) would you like to see in a future book?

_____

(Survey questions continue on next page.)

3. Where did you purchase this book? (If you borrowed it from a library, please give the name of the library.)

_____

4. What influenced your decision to read this book?

_____Front Cover   _____First Page   _____Back Cover Copy

_____Title   _____Friends

_____Publicity (Please describe)_____

_____

5. Please indicate your age range:

_____Under 18   _____25-34   _____46-55

_____18-24   _____35-45   _____Over 55

If desired, include additional comments below.